THE S

Holly licked her dry lips, wishing Belinda and Tracy were there with her.

The blood sang in her ears, but otherwise the night was completely silent. There was not a single sound from the armoury. Whatever Lucy was doing there, she was doing it in total silence.

At last Holly couldn't stand it any more. She prised herself out of her hiding-place and edged her head round the open doorway.

Holly's mouth fell open in surprise and her eyes grew as round as saucers.

The armoury was completely deserted. Lucy had vanished!

The Mystery Club series

1. Secret Clues
2. Double Danger
3. The Forbidden Island
4. Mischief at Midnight
5. Dangerous Tricks
6. Missing!
7. Hide and Seek
8. Buried Secrets
9. Deadly Games
10. Crossed Lines
11. Dark Horse
12. Deceptions
13. Fatal Fall
14. Crash Landing
15. Poison!
16. Out of Control
17. The Secret Room

The Secret Room
The Mystery Club 17

Fiona Kelly

*Hodder
Children's
Books*

a division of Hodder Headline plc

Special thanks to Allan Frewin Jones and Sue Welford

Copyright © Ben M. Baglio 1995
Created by Ben M. Baglio, W6 0HE

First published in Great Britain in 1995
by Hodder Children's Books

The right of Fiona Kelly to be identified as the Author of
the Work has been asserted by her in accordance with the
Copyright, Designs and Patents Act 1988.

10 9 8 7 6 5 4 3 2 1

All rights reserved. No part of this publication may be
reproduced, stored in a retrieval system, or transmitted,
in any form or by any means without the prior written
permission of the publisher, nor be otherwise circulated
in any form of binding or cover other than that in which
it is published and without a similar condition being
imposed on the subsequent purchaser.

All characters in this publication are fictitious and any
resemblance to real persons, living or dead, is purely
coincidental.

A Catalogue record for this book is
available from the British Library

ISBN 0 340 63613 0

Typeset by Hewer Text Composition Services, Edinburgh

Printed and bound in Great Britain by
Cox and Wyman Ltd, Reading, Berks

Hodder Children's Books
A division of Hodder Headline plc
338 Euston Road
London NW1 3BH

1 Abandoned

'Oh! *Help!*'

Holly Adams let out a yell as a single move forward sent her tumbling into the deep, dark mine-shaft.

'That serves you right,' Belinda Hayes said unfeelingly. 'You shouldn't have laughed at me when I got stuck in that quicksand!'

'My move!' said Tracy Foster, scooping the dice off the board and giving them a good shake in both cupped hands.

Holly glanced through the train carriage window.

'The sea!' she exclaimed. 'Look!'

The three friends gazed out into the rosy light of the early evening. A beautiful red sunset sent soft splashes of orange and gold over the sea, creating a picture that was like something out of a fairy tale.

'Wow!' said Tracy. 'I'm impressed.' It was as if the

rolling green Yorkshire fields had simply winked out of existence. Last time the three friends had looked out of the window, they had been travelling through the rich, undulating countryside. Now all they could see to their left was the crimson sky and the smooth blue of the endless sea.

Belinda pressed her nose against the glass and looked down. The railway track ran along the edge of a tall cliff. A single step from the speeding train would have sent her plunging down a sheer drop to the hidden shoreline below.

'We're almost there,' Belinda said as she hauled down the window in the door and stuck her head out. The wind whipped her unruly brown hair and almost tore her wire-framed glasses off her round, grinning face.

'Rymarsh dead ahead!' she shouted.

'Show me,' said Tracy, forcing her head out beside Belinda's. Belinda had to duck back out of the way as the slipstream sent Tracy's blonde hair flying into her face.

The cliff made a long, slow downwards curve towards a distant town nestled in a gloriously picturesque bay.

'Holly, come and look at this!' said Tracy, her voice taking on the excited twang that gave away her American upbringing. 'It's out of this world!'

Holly clambered over Belinda and looked out of the open window.

'It's called Wrath Bay,' said Belinda as she struggled to see through a window already filled with the craning heads of Holly and Tracy. 'If you had a pair of binoculars you'd probably be able to see Wylde House. Hey? Pals? Excuse me, can I have a look, too? I mean, we wouldn't *be* here if it wasn't for me.'

'You mean if it wasn't for your mom and dad,' said Tracy as she pulled back into the carriage.

'Yeah!' Belinda said with a grin. She lifted a can of Coke in a mock toast. 'Here's to important business trips abroad.'

Mr Hayes, Belinda's father, was often called on to attend business meetings in other countries. But it was less usual for him to be called away to a week-long function such as the one taking place in Geneva; a convention which included grand dinners and balls, and to which the families of those attending were also invited with five-star hotel accommodation included.

Easy-going, jeans-and-sweat-shirt Belinda had made it very clear to her parents that she would rather spend a week buried up to her neck in a compost heap than be dragged around in expensive dresses making small-talk with a lot of boring people she didn't know.

A business associate of her father's, a man called John Fanshaw, came to Belinda's rescue by inviting her to stay with him and his wife and daughter at their house on the cliffs that lifted their rugged shoulders over the coastal town of Rymarsh. And it didn't take long for Belinda to arrange for the invitation to be stretched to include her two best friends and fellow members of the Mystery Club, Holly and Tracy.

Holly closed the window and the three friends began to clear up the debris of their long journey. There were crisp packets and apple cores and empty drinks cans to be gathered for later disposal. And there was the board-game to fold up and put away.

It was a game that the three of them had invented. They had drawn out the playing board themselves on a large sheet of paper and had glued it on to an old draughts board. They called their game The Mystery Chase. It worked like any normal board game, with tokens and dice and squares that did everything from trapping you in a locked room until you threw a six, to providing you with a helicopter in which you could fly ten squares forward.

Holly had the uncanny tendency to win the

game and find the secret documents while her two friends were still trapped in mines or caught in quicksand, which was why Belinda hadn't been sympathetic when Holly's last move had sent her down a mine-shaft.

To prevent arguments when they resumed the game later, Tracy made a note of where everyone's tokens were and whose throw came next. Then they spent the last five minutes of their journey perched excitedly on the edge of their seats with their cases and bags piled around them, waiting for the train to pull into Rymarsh station.

'So what are the Fanshaws like?' Holly asked Belinda. 'And what's Lucy like?'

Lucy was John and Susan Fanshaw's eighteen year old daughter.

'Susan and John always seemed nice enough when we visited them or when they came to see us,' said Belinda. 'Lucy wasn't with them very often, though. She went to boarding school. I've only met her a couple of times and she never paid much attention to me, so I don't really know what she's like. My mum says she's a bit wild.'

'Wild?' said Tracy. 'What kind of wild?'

'Oh, you know,' said Belinda with a shrug. 'The typical spoilt little rich kid stuff, I suppose.'

'You mean like you?' said Tracy with a grin.

'I was never *spoilt*,' said Belinda. 'And when have I ever behaved like a rich kid?'

Tracy eyed Belinda's baggy old green sweat-shirt and faded blue jeans.

'If there's one thing Belinda *can't* be accused of,' Holly laughed, 'it's behaving like a rich kid.'

'That's right,' said Belinda. 'I can't help it if my parents are loaded. *I'm* perfectly normal.'

'I know,' said Tracy. 'I was only kidding. And just think, if your folks weren't rich and important, they wouldn't be in Geneva right now, and we wouldn't be having this great holiday.'

The three girls had been firm friends ever since Tracy and Belinda had responded to an advert which Holly had put into the school magazine. Holly's plan had been to form a club dedicated to reading and discussing the mystery books she loved. What she hadn't expected was that the three of them would find themselves involved in real life mysteries! But that was exactly what happened. Sometimes it seemd that Holly Adams was an absolute magnet for mysteries.

The railway line descended slowly from the giddy heights of the cliff edge and their train slowed as it approached the quiet old town of Rymarsh.

No one else got off the train as the three friends hauled their luggage out on to the platform.

'What a quiet place,' said Holly as they carried their bags to the exit. There was no one in attendance at the station and once the train had drawn away, it seemed as though there might not be another living person in the entire town.

'Do you think anyone actually lives here?' said Tracy. 'I mean, what is this? A ghost town or something?'

The twilight was gathering as they brought their cases out into the deserted carpark that fronted the railway station.

Holly took a deep breath, her nostrils filling with the sharp, evocative smell of the sea.

'Susan said she'd be waiting,' said Belinda, dumping her bags and staring across the empty stretch of grey tarmac. Beyond a wire fence the buildings of the town climbed a steep hill.

A few people walked past and the stillness was broken by the occasional passing car. The three friends looked hopefully towards the entrance of the carpark at the sound of each approaching car. But none came through the gates.

Belinda looked at her watch. They had been standing there for fifteen minutes.

'I wish these little stations still had full-time staff,' said Belinda. 'At least then there'd be someone to ask.'

'To ask what?' said Tracy.

'I don't know,' Belinda said with a hint of irritation in her voice. 'To ask the way to Wylde House, as it looks like we're going to have to walk there at this rate.' Wylde House was the name of the place where Susan and John Fanshaw lived.

'Don't you know the way?' asked Holly. 'I thought you said you'd been here before.'

'I have,' said Belinda. 'By car, and not from this direction. All I remember is that the road crosses a kind of causeway between the river and the sea. And then there's a bridge and a steep road up to the house. Wylde House! If someone doesn't pick us up pretty soon, it won't just be the house that's wild! I'm starving.'

'I tell you what,' said Holly. 'There's a newsagent's shop just over the road. You two stay here and I'll nip across. I'll get us something to eat and ask if there's a bus or something that'll take us near Wylde House. Give me a shout if Susan turns up.'

Holly ran across the road.

'Are they always this unreliable?' asked Tracy.

'Don't ask me,' said Belinda. 'I've never had to rely on them for anything before.' She looked at her watch again. 'I'm positive Susan said she'd be here with the car to pick us up. We worked out the train times and everything.'

'Maybe she's got a flat tyre,' said Tracy. She grinned as she looked along the empty street. 'Or maybe she got caught in traffic.'

'Hmm!' Belinda wasn't in the mood to be amused by Tracy's daft joke. She was more concerned with what they were going to do if Susan Fanshaw didn't turn up at all. She'd mentioned walking, but even if they knew the way, they wouldn't be able to drag their cases all the way.

Holly came running back with her hands full of sweet and chocolate bars.

'Come on,' she said. 'I've arranged a lift. The husband of the woman in the shop runs the local taxi service. She said it's only a ten-minute drive.'

'What if Susan turns up when we've gone?' said Tracy. 'Shouldn't we leave her a note or something?'

'She'll figure out what's happened,' said Belinda. 'She'll realise that once we knew we'd been abandoned, we'd find our own way to the house. Besides, we may even pass her on the way. There's only one road to Wylde House.'

'I don't imagine she's actually abandoned us,' said Holly as they picked up their bags and walked across the road towards the newsagent's shop. 'Something must have happened to delay her.'

'That's exactly what I said,' added Tracy.

'Yeah, maybe,' Belinda said crossly. 'But if we get there and find them all sitting watching television with their feet up, I shan't be amused, I can tell you that. This is supposed to be a holiday, not an initiative test.'

A few moments later a sleek four-door saloon came to a halt at the kerb and a cheerful face smiled at them through the driver's open window.

'Party of three to Wylde House, is it?' said the middle-aged man. He got out to help them cram their luggage into the boot.

'Do you know the Fanshaws at all?' asked Belinda as she climbed into the front passenger seat.

'I know young Lucy,' said the man. 'I used to be forever going up to the house to take her out on her jaunts.' He glanced over his shoulder to check that Tracy and Holly were strapped in. 'That was before she got her own car, of course. I don't see much of her now, except when she whistles by at seventy miles an hour in that sports car of hers.' He started the car and it glided smoothly along the street. 'Are you friends of Miss Lucy, then?'

'Not really,' said Belinda. 'My dad does business with John Fanshaw. We're staying here for a week while my parents are away.'

'A week?' said the man. 'So you'll be here for the Children's Masquerade on Saturday?'

'What's the Children's Masquerade?' asked Belinda. 'I've never heard of it.'

Holly and Tracy leaned forwards to listen.

'Mrs Fanshaw will tell you all about it,' said the driver. 'It's the biggest event of the year in this neck of the woods.' He laughed. 'Some people say it's the only event.' The car turned a bend and they found themselves heading away from the little town. 'You ask Mrs Fanshaw all about it. It's tied in with the history of Wylde House, and the legend of Sir Brandon's lost treasure, and of the Lady.'

'What lady?' asked Holly, her ears pricking up at the mention of hidden treasure. Holly loved mysteries, and there were few things more mysterious than legends of lost treasure.

'The Lady of Wrath,' the driver said. 'You ask Mrs Fanshaw.'

The car rose up a shallow incline and the girls found themselves on the narrow causeway which Belinda had mentioned. To the right they could see the brown waters of the River Wrath, the water low between muddy banks as it ran with the outgoing tide.

To the left, a shallow sandy beach stretched to the foaming tide. The last traces of copper-coloured sunlight glinted on the crests of the incoming waves. A little way out to sea something large and dark reared ominously out of the water.

'I remember that!' cried Belinda. She looked round at her two friends. 'It's a ruined old watch tower. You can walk to it at low tide, but when the tide is right up, it's completely cut off.'

'Who'd build a watch tower right out in the sea?' asked Tracy, gazing at the ragged-edged lump of blackness lapped by the receding tide.

'It wasn't in the sea when it was built,' said the driver. 'And that old ruin was the east tower of Wrath Castle. A great big castle, it was, in the old days before the storm that tore down the cliff and let the sea in.'

'When was that?' asked Holly.

'Oh, a long time ago,' said the driver. 'The castle fell into the sea in the Middle Ages. That tower is all that's left of it.'

The car drove up over a small hump-backed bridge where the River Wrath fed into the sea. The three girls saw the steep rise of the hill in front of them.

'The house is right at the top here,' said Belinda. 'We're almost there.'

Tracy and Holly stared in amazement as the car climbed the hill road and the outlines of Wylde House rose into sight.

'You call that a *house*?' breathed Tracy.

'It's like a palace!' said Holly.

Wylde House certainly was an imposing building, especially when seen against the backdrop of a purple evening sky. Long red-brick wings spread out from the main building with its stone-carved decorations and lancet windows. The high walls were edged with a checker-work of cream stones and topped by ornamental battlements, beyond which the slopes of the slate roofs were visible. Huge red-brick chimney stacks rose into the sky.

'You didn't say it was this big,' said Tracy, leaning over Belinda's shoulder to get a better look.

'Didn't I?' said Belinda with a grin. 'Maybe I wanted to surprise you. And this isn't all of it. There's a chapel around the back, and gardens with fountains and statues and things.' She smiled at her friends. 'Didn't I say this was going to be a holiday to remember?'

The driver took the car round to the impressive front door of the house and helped the three of them take their luggage out of the boot.

Belinda paid the driver and the three of them carried their cases to the broad step that led to the front door.

'OK,' said Belinda, pressing the brass doorbell.

'Let's see what excuses they manage to come up with.'

The door was opened by a woman whom Holly imagined to be in her forties. She was dressed in casual but obviously expensive clothes, her light brown hair carefully styled round a slim attractive face.

'Belinda! At last. I was beginning to think you'd missed your train,' said Susan Fanshaw with a relieved expression on her face. She smiled at Holly and Tracy and then looked puzzled as her eyes went past them. 'Where's Lucy?'

'Lucy?' said Belinda. 'I'm sorry, what do you mean?'

Susan Fanshaw's face fell. 'Didn't Lucy pick you up at the station?'

Belinda shook her head. ''Fraid not,' she said. 'Was she supposed to?'

'Of course she was,' said Susan. 'John had to borrow my car because his own one is in the garage, so I asked Lucy to meet you in her car.' Holly thought Susan sounded more angry than worried about her missing daughter. 'That girl!' she said.

'It's OK,' Holly said brightly, 'really it is. We got a taxi.'

'That's not the point,' Susan said grimly. 'Lucy

promised to pick you up. I'll have something to say to her when she gets home!' Susan's face brightened. 'I'm sorry. As if you haven't had enough to put up with, here I am leaving you standing on the doorstep. Come in, all of you. Come in and welcome to Wylde House. I'm sorry there's been such an inauspicious start to your holiday. I'll show you straight to your rooms and by the time you've unpacked, dinner will be ready. I expect you'll be hungry after that long journey.'

'Pretty hungry,' agreed Belinda, temporarily forgetting the chocolate she'd wolfed in the taxi. Susan Fanshaw ushered them into the house and closed the door.

The hall was overwhelming; all oak panelling and marble tiles with great brooding paintings hanging on the walls. A wide stairway led to a dark-oak gallery, lined with more paintings.

Holly and Tracy stared about them in astonishment as they were led up the stairs. It was all so much grander than Belinda had led them to believe. True, she had told them that it was a Tudor house, but she certainly hadn't revealed quite how imposing it would be.

But even as they were taken along an oak-panelled corridor to their bedrooms, Holly couldn't help wondering exactly what had happened to Lucy Fanshaw.

Had she simply forgotten to meet them, as her mother plainly believed, or was there some other reason why the young woman had been unable to be at the railway station that evening?

2 An angry exchange

Holly couldn't quite believe her eyes as she found herself in her bedroom. The walls were lined with glowing oak and the high ceiling was a mass of ivory-coloured plaster carvings. She dropped her case and threw herself on to the four-poster bed with a breathless shout of laughter.

She gazed up at the ornate ceiling for a few moments before rolling off the bed and running to look out of the mullioned window with its heavy velvet curtains. In the darkness she found herself staring out over expansive lawns. To one side a dark shape declared itself as some kind of smallish building. Holly remembered Belinda's mention of a chapel.

'I bet this place is just full of mysteries and legends,' Holly breathed, as she stared in delight through the window. 'I can't wait to start exploring!'

'That's the first sign of madness, you know,' said Belinda. Holly turned and saw that her friend had come quietly into her room.

'What is?' asked Holly.

'Talking to yourself,' Belinda said with a smile.

'Are you sure talking to you isn't the first sign?' said Holly. She smiled at her friend. 'This is an amazing place.' She gestured out into the darkness. 'Does all this land belong to the house?'

'As far as the eye can see,' said Belinda. 'Depending on what direction you're looking in, of course. They certainly own everything between here and the sea.'

'Hey, guys, wait 'til you get a look at the room they've given me,' Tracy exclaimed, running into Holly's room with eyes like saucers. 'Oh! Yours is the same. Isn't it totally amazing? My bed looks like it ought to have a sign on it: Queen Elizabeth the First slept here.'

'She certainly could have done,' said Susan Fanshaw from the doorway. 'This house was built during the reign of Henry the Eighth. Elizabeth was his daughter, you know.'

'That's right,' said Belinda. 'She was Anne Boleyn's daughter. The one who got her head chopped off.'

'Queen Elizabeth got her head chopped off?' said Tracy. 'Are you sure?'

'No, silly,' said Belinda. 'Her *mum* did. And then Henry got married again, to—'

'Before you start the history lesson, Belinda,' interrupted Susan, 'I think I ought to mention that dinner is just about ready for you.'

Belinda's eyes lit up.

Before they went into the dining-room, Holly and Tracy quickly phoned home to let their parents know they had arrived safely, and to give enthusiastic descriptions of Wylde House.

They ate off a polished wooden table at one end of a long hall hung with tapestries and filled with antique furniture.

'I'm sorry John can't be here to welcome you,' said Susan as Belinda helped her lift dishes from the hostess trolley. 'He won't be back for an hour or two yet. And I'm especially sorry that Lucy isn't here. I can't believe how thoughtlessly she's behaved. She promised to meet you at the station.'

'You don't think something's happened to her, do you?' Holly asked cautiously.

Susan snorted. 'I doubt that,' she said. 'If the car had broken down she'd have been on the phone for help. And if there had been an accident, we'd have heard by now. No, she just forgot, knowing her. Her mind's too full of that—' Susan's voice came to a sudden halt, as if she had been about to tell some secret about Lucy but had stopped herself in time.

There were a few moments of awkward silence as Susan Fanshaw glowered angrily at her plate.

Holly was sure of one thing: she wouldn't like to be in Lucy's shoes when she did finally turn up.

'What's the Children's Masquerade?' Tracy asked Susan, deliberately changing the subject. 'The taxi driver told us to ask you about it.'

'He said it was going on this weekend,' said Belinda.

'That's right,' said Susan. 'It's just a bit of fun, but it takes a fair amount of organising, I can tell you. There's going to be a small funfair and sideshows and a firework display. And a torchlight parade down to the Wrath to give thanks. It's all taking place in the grounds on Saturday.'

'To give thanks for what?' asked Holly.

'It's a long story,' said Susan.

'I like long stories,' said Holly.

'Well,' began Susan, 'it all goes back to the Civil War, when Oliver Cromwell's Parliamentarian Army was fighting against King Charles the First. The King's forces had been beaten near here and were in full retreat. Cromwell's army had been looting the countryside and news reached the house that a large force was heading this way. They knew what that meant. At the very least the house would be stripped of all its treasures, and at worst everyone would be put to the sword. At that time the house was owned by Sir Brandon Wylde and his wife, the Lady Eleanor, and they were staunch supporters of the King. Now, most of the local menfolk had left to join the King's army, and Sir Brandon was at a loss as to how to defend the house.

'As Cromwell's army approached,' Susan continued, 'the women and children of Rymarsh fled to the sanctuary of the house. Sir Brandon knew they had one natural ally – the causeway. It was narrower in those days and no more than three men could cross it side by side. Which meant that no army would be able to attack successfully from that direction as long as even a small force opposed them. And the army couldn't reach the house any other way because to the north and east were the cliffs and to the south the valley bottom was all marshland under the steep slope of the hill.'

The three girls listened in thrilled silence as the tale unfolded.

'While Lady Eleanor set about hiding the silver and gold,' continued Susan, 'Sir Brandon got the women and children from the town to put on helmets from the armoury and stand at the windows of the house so that from a distance it would look as if there was a large force of soldiers waiting there. The

Parliamentarians arrived late at night. Under the cover of darkness, Sir Brandon took his ceremonial sword and marched down to the causeway with a few of the older children dressed as soldiers. He stepped out on to the causeway and stood there with his sword in his hands, barring the way.'

'Wow!' gasped Tracy. 'Talk about brave. What happened next?'

'The Parliamentarians came creeping across the causeway,' said Susan. 'But Sir Brandon held his ground. He convinced them that Wylde House was heavily guarded and that if they dared take one step on to his land not one of them would ever return home alive.'

'And they fell for it?' said Belinda. 'That's totally brilliant!'

Susan smiled. 'They fell for it, all right. In the light of the burning torches they didn't realise Sir Brandon was only backed up by a gang of children. And the Parliamentarians couldn't afford to waste time fighting to take Wylde House. They had to get back to the main army and pursue the retreating Royalists. So they went away and Wylde House was saved.'

'But Cromwell won the Civil War in the end, didn't he?' said Belinda. 'What happened to the house afterwards?'

'That's the sad part of the story,' said Susan. 'The whole of the local area was infected with the plague shortly afterwards. Sir Brandon died, and so did Lady Eleanor.'

'That's rotten,' said Holly. 'Fancy dying of some disease after all that! And I suppose the Parliamentarians just walked in and took all the treasures, did they?'

'That's probably what happened, yes,' said Susan. 'But we do have a legend that Lady Eleanor hid the treasures so well that not one gold coin nor one silver candlestick was ever found.'

'Excuse me,' said Holly, sensing a mystery. 'When you say ever, do you mean not even to this day?'

Susan laughed. 'That's right,' she said. 'The legend says that there is a priest's hole somewhere in this house, and that if anyone was ever able to discover it, they'd find it crammed with Lady Eleanor's lost treasure.' Susan shook her head. 'But I don't believe it exists. It's much more likely that Cromwell's men found the treasures and took them away centuries ago. But it's a nice legend.'

'What's a priest's hole?' asked Tracy. 'Is it, like, a hole in the ground, or something?'

'It's a secret room,' said Susan. 'A lot of houses built in Tudor times had secret compartments where priests could hide. You see, Henry the Eighth had split England away from the Church of Rome, and anyone who disapproved was liable to get into a lot of trouble. So families that secretly didn't agree with what Henry was doing would hide priests from him.'

'Could we see this priest's hole?' asked Tracy.

Susan laughed. 'You could if anyone had the faintest clue where it was,' she said. 'Or even if it really exists. I've lived in this house for the last twenty years, and I've never come across it.'

'It'll be really well hidden, I bet,' said Holly, her eyes shining. 'Would it be OK for us to try and find it?'

'You're very welcome to search the place from the attics to the cellars, if you fancy it,' said Susan. 'But I don't think you'll find anything. If the secret's remained undiscovered for the past three hundred years, I don't really think it's likely to come to light in the next few days.'

'But *I* haven't been looking before,' said Holly. 'If there's a secret room in this house, I'm going to find it.'

Susan smiled at the determination in Holly's voice.

'She means it,' said Belinda. 'Once Holly gets an idea in her head, you can't get it out with a crowbar. If there's a priest's hole, she'll find it, all right. She'll probably find the priest, as well.'

'But not tonight,' Tracy said with a yawn. 'Oh! I'm sorry, but I'm really tired.'

'You can't go to bed yet,' said Belinda. 'Susan hasn't finished her story.'

'I have, really,' said Susan. 'After the restoration of the monarchy, the house was taken over by another family, and it was they who started the annual pageant of the Children's Masquerade. And it's been held on this coming weekend more or less every year since. As I said, there'll be a funfair, a masked dance, fireworks and a torchlit procession of children in Tudor clothes down to the causeway. And John will take the traditional role of Sir Brandon, and he'll carry the very same sword that Sir Brandon carried.'

'The sword still exists?' said Holly.

'Oh, yes,' said Susan. 'Lady Eleanor's treasure might be a fairy story, but the Lady of Wrath is real enough.'

'The Lady of Wrath?' said Belinda. 'Who's she?'

'It's not a *she*,' said Susan. 'It's an *it*. The sword that Sir Brandon carried when he saw off Cromwell's army is called the Lady of Wrath. For fifty-one weeks of the year it's on loan to a local museum, but traditionally it lies on Sir Brandon's tomb for seven nights before the Children's Masquerade. Which is where it is now. In our chapel. You'll be able to see it tomorrow. It's very impressive.'

Holly was about to ask how the sword came to have such an odd name when there was the sound of the front door opening.

Susan got up from the table.

'John?' she called. 'Lucy?'

'It's me, Susan,' called a man's deep voice. John Fanshaw came striding into the dining-room. He was a tall, ruggedly handsome man with a swept-back mane of greying hair and piercing black eyes.

He greeted the three girls, shaking each of them in turn firmly by the hand whilst apologising for his late arrival. He started asking Belinda a few polite questions about her parents.

'Could I have a quick word, John?' Susan asked, taking him by the arm and steering him out into the hallway.

'He seems a nice guy,' whispered Tracy.

There was a muffled exclamation of anger from the hall.

'Oops,' said Belinda. 'I think Susan's just told him about Lucy.'

The three girls could hear a heated but subdued debate going on out in the hall.

'You've been here before,' Holly said to Belinda. 'Whereabouts do you think the priest's hole could be?'

'I haven't a clue,' said Belinda. 'Don't forget I've only been here with my parents. I had to sit quietly in a corner and behave myself. I've never explored the place.'

'That's just what I'd like to do tomorrow,' said Holly. 'First thing in the morning. If we don't find that secret room by the time we leave then my name's not Holly Adams.'

Tracy got up and walked over to the window, her hand stroking the soft plush of the folded curtains as she looked out into the well of the night.

'I'd like to explore that old watch tower as well,' she said. 'And the cliffs. We're going to have such a brilliant time here! Hey – I can see some lights out there.' She curled her hand against the glass to block out the light from the room. In the shadow of her hand she saw twin lights moving closer up the hill. In a couple of moments a car slewed into view and came to a halt on the front drive.

'What sort of car does Lucy drive?' asked Tracy as an attractive young woman with extraordinarily long ash-blonde hair climbed out of the car.

'Some sort of sports car,' said Belinda.

'Then I think she's home,' said Tracy.

The other two ran to the window. The young woman was dressed in a white blouse and white jeans, a white silk scarf flying at her throat as she strode purposefully towards the front door.

'This could be nasty,' said Belinda. 'I think we'd better keep out of sight.'

They heard the front door open.

'Lucy!' cried Susan. 'Where on earth have you been?'

'Out!' Lucy's voice sounded shrill, as if she was either upset or very angry.

'Don't speak to your mother in that tone of voice,' demanded John Fanshaw. 'You were supposed to pick up Belinda Hayes and her friends from the station. They had to take a taxi in the end.'

'I had other things on my mind,' said Lucy. 'What's the big problem? They got here all right, didn't they? What do you think I am, a chauffeur?'

'She sounds a real charmer,' murmured Tracy. 'I'm glad she didn't pick us up.'

'I know she was supposed to be a bit wilful,' whispered Belinda as the three girls kept themselves discreetly hidden in the dining-room. 'But I didn't think she'd be this bad.'

'Control yourself!' John Fanshaw demanded. 'This is all the influence of that lad. Have you been seeing him again against my express wishes?'

'Yes, I have,' shouted Lucy. 'But don't you worry, Dad, I shan't be seeing him again. I shan't ever see him again, thanks to you. I suppose it was you who told his father that we should be stopped from seeing each other?'

'I did it for your own good,' said John. 'I told his father to have a quiet word with him.'

'Oh, he did that, all right,' shouted Lucy. 'He's sent Colin away. And it's all your fault.'

'Sent him away?' asked Susan. 'Lucy, what do you mean?'

'Colin left for Manchester this evening,' said Lucy. 'His father's sent him to live with his mother. I've just come from the railway station. And I hope you're both satisfied, because you've ruined my life!' There was the hammering of feet on the stairs.

'Lucy!' called John. 'Come back down here!'

'No!'

Holly and her friends looked at each other.

'Crumbs,' whispered Belinda. 'How embarrassing!'

'Leave her, John,' they heard Susan say. 'She's upset. We can talk to her about it in the morning.'

Her voice lowered to a warning hiss that was still audible to the three friends. 'And we've got guests, don't forget.'

The Fanshaws came back into the dining-room. Susan said a few weak things about Lucy being upset as a place was set at the table for John and the meal was resumed.

Tracy was yawning behind her hand again within half an hour and it wasn't much later when the excitement of the day began to tell on Holly and Belinda as well. The three friends said goodnight to John and Susan and headed up for bed.

The bathroom was at the far end of the corridor where they had their rooms. Holly was the last to wash and clean her teeth. She came out of the bathroom and very nearly collided with Lucy Fanshaw.

'Oh!' exclaimed Lucy. 'Hello, there. Don't tell me. You must be either Tracy or Holly.'

'I'm Holly,' said Holly, surprised by the cheerful expression on the young woman's face.

'Pleased to meet you,' said Lucy amiably. 'I'm sorry about the mess-up with the station, but I had to do something really important.'

'That's OK,' said Holly. 'We found our own way here.'

'Great,' said Lucy with a broad smile. 'Is the bathroom free?'

Holly nodded and Lucy went sweeping past her. The door closed and Holly was amazed to hear Lucy start singing to herself.

Holly stared at the closed door for a moment before padding off to her bedroom.

What a strange girl, Holly thought as she climbed into bed. *One minute she's talking about her life being ruined, and the next minute she's acting like she's won the lottery.*

Holly pulled the blankets up over her ears. One thing was for sure: no matter how upset Lucy had seemed when she'd been talking to her parents, the truth of what was going on with her and the boy called Colin was very different from what she'd said.

3 The Lady of Wrath

Holly wasn't sure what woke her in the silent darkness of deepest night. For a moment or two she felt confused. Even in the gloom she could tell that all the contours and shapes around her were wrong. And her bed felt wrong as well.

And then she remembered. She wasn't in her own bedroom in the small Yorkshire town of Willow Dale. She was in a four-poster bed in an oak-panelled room in a huge Tudor house high on the cliffs overlooking Wrath Bay.

If the silence of the night had not been so complete, Holly would never have heard the small, distant tapping noise that came from outside her window. Intrigued, she slid out of bed and padded across the floor. She lifted an edge of the heavy curtain aside and peered out. The black sky was ablaze with stars. In the distance a single, steady line of stars cut across the horizon.

That's strange, thought Holly, rubbing her eyes.

And then she realised what it was that she was looking at. The line of stars had to be the lights of fishing boats on the rim of the sea. Holly shivered at the thought of being out there on the cold North Sea while everyone else was snug in bed. She didn't envy those fishermen one little bit.

She was about to go back to bed when a movement much closer to the house caught her attention. Someone was standing in the deep shadow of the building which she assumed to be the chapel. She narrowed her eyes to try and see better, but all she could make out was the outline of a shoulder, a head and an arm. If not for the fact that she had seen it move, she'd have assumed it was just a statue standing at the corner of the chapel wall.

Holly was sharp-witted enough, even at that time of night, to realise that no one should be lurking out there – at least, no one with good intent. Could it be a burglar?

But before Holly had time to pursue her thoughts any further she saw a flash of oddly coloured light. An arched oblong of multicoloured light in the wall of the chapel. It was a window; a light from within the chapel itself, shining through a pattern of coloured glass.

The light faded from the first window only to

glow out of the next arch along. Someone was walking along inside the chapel holding a light of some sort.

The figure outside the chapel moved swiftly. Holly saw a narrow crack of yellow light. A door was being opened. The figure slid in through the crack and the door closed again. But in those few moments Holly had seen that the moving light came from a torch, and, stranger yet, that the person holding the torch had a long fall of ash-blonde hair.

There was no doubt in Holly's mind as to who she had seen. It was Lucy Fanshaw. And it didn't take a genius to guess who it was that she was letting into the chapel. It had to be the young man called Colin.

Holly watched as the torch lit up the narrow coloured windows along the chapel. And then, quite suddenly, the light went out.

Holly waited with bated breath for five minutes or more but there was no further sign of life from within the chapel.

Well, she thought, *no wonder Lucy wasn't upset when I saw her. Her boyfriend hasn't gone to Manchester at all. He's right here.*

Holly went back to bed. She had a problem to wrestle with. Should she tell Susan what she had seen or should she just keep quiet about it and mind her own business?

She snuggled under the blankets.

I'll talk to Tracy and Belinda about it in the morning, she thought drowsily. *Between the three of us, we'll work out what's best*.

A few minutes later Holly was fast asleep.

As soon as she had washed and dressed Holly went along to Tracy's room, catching her in the middle of one of her early morning exercise regimes.

'I've already been for a run out in the grounds,' Tracy puffed, lying on her back and bicycling her legs in the air. 'This is just a top-up.'

She brought her legs down and bounced to her feet, her face glowing with health.

'I went right to the cliff edge,' said Tracy. 'That ruined tower looks totally brilliant in daylight. The tide's out. I bet we could walk there and back easily before the tide came back in. What do you say?'

'Not right now,' said Holly. 'Come with me and we'll wake Belinda up. I've got something to tell you both.'

Tracy knocked on Belinda's door.

'C'mon, lazybones!' she called. 'I've been up and out already. I'll bet you're not even out of bed.'

'Oh, yes I am,' came a sleepy voice from beyond

the door. 'I've been up for ages. I've already been down to the beach in my swimming togs. I've done a couple of lengths of the bay, *and* I ran all the way back up the hill.'

'In your dreams!' said Tracy, opening the door. Belinda's room was in darkness, but they could see that she was still tucked up in bed.

'Dreams?' said Belinda, sitting up and putting her spectacles on. 'That would have been a nightmare! What do you two want at this time of day? You're not dragging me out on any route marches before breakfast, I can tell you that much.'

Holly drew the curtains open. She stood with her back to the sunshine-filled window.

'Have I got news for you two!' she said dramatically.

The three of them sat on the bed while Holly recounted all that she had seen the previous night.

'Wow,' said Tracy. 'A midnight assignation. That is so romantic!'

'Never mind romantic,' said Holly. 'Lucy was letting someone into the chapel. It must have been that boy they had the argument about. What I want to know is, should we tell Susan and John?'

'Hmm,' Belinda murmured thoughtfully. 'That'll get Lucy into even more trouble. I don't know,

Holly. I think we should keep out of it. Unless, of course, we go downstairs and find the place has been ransacked in the night.'

'It hasn't been,' said Tracy. 'I think I'd have noticed when I went down earlier.'

'Besides,' said Belinda. 'Lucy wasn't letting him into the house. You said she let him into the chapel. It's a separate building.'

'It is?' said Holly. 'Then where did they go when the light went off?'

'Maybe they went into another room in the chapel. Or perhaps they simply didn't want to draw attention to the chapel by keeping the light on,' said Belinda. 'Look, Holly, haven't we got enough things to keep us occupied this week, without you getting us involved in Lucy Fanshaw's comings and goings?'

'I suppose you're right,' said Holly. 'I just don't like the idea of Susan and John not knowing what she's up to. How are we going to feel if . . . if . . . well, if the pair of them have eloped in the night?'

Belinda clambered out of bed. 'Tell you what, Holly,' she said. 'If it turns out that they've run off together, then you can tell Susan all about it. Otherwise,' Belinda made a zipping motion across her lips, 'we keep quiet, OK?'

Having agreed on this, the three friends went downstairs in search of some breakfast.

They found Susan in the large quarry-tiled kitchen.

'Good morning,' Susan said. 'Did you all sleep well?'

'Like logs,' said Belinda.

'That's the sea air,' Susan said with a laugh. 'There's a fridge full of food. I'm sure I can leave you to sort out your own breakfasts, I've got some phone-calls to make. We're planning on having one of those bouncy castle things on Saturday, and I want to make sure it arrives on time.'

'Can we make something to eat for you and John?' asked Holly.

'I've eaten, thanks,' said Susan. 'And John is halfway to Birmingham by now.' She smiled. 'He won't be back until Friday night. I'd accuse him of doing it on purpose to get out of helping me arrange Saturday's do, if I didn't know he *had* to be away.' She squared her shoulders. 'Still, everything's going fine so far.' She tapped her head. 'Touch wood! You three can keep yourselves amused, can't you? I'd ask Lucy to show you round, but I'd rather not get into another argument with her after last night.'

'She did seem a little upset,' said Tracy.

Susan sighed. 'It's all very boring stuff, I'm afraid. Lucy has been offered a place at Exeter University, but she's been seeing this boy recently and her latest plan is to give up going to university to be with him. John hit the roof, of course. I've tried reasoning with her, you know, telling her that three years isn't for ever, but once Lucy makes her mind up she can be as stubborn as a mule.'

Susan gave a tired smile. 'There's still a couple of months before term starts. I'm just hoping she comes to her senses by then. Maybe things will calm down now that Colin has been sent away to live with his mother. I certainly hope so.'

Holly felt a twinge of conscience. If her guess was right and the boy let into the chapel last night was Colin, then it was unlikely that things would calm down with Lucy.

Belinda made the three of them scrambled eggs on toast. As soon as they had eaten and washed up they headed out into the grounds for their first real look round. The land around Wylde House rose out of the countryside in one big curved hill. Near the house it was all lawns and neat flower-beds and geometric herb gardens, but on the slopes of the hill behind the house there were tall trees and a mass of undergrowth.

The hill was cut off to the east and the north by tall cliffs.

'Come with me,' said Tracy, running across the lawn. 'Last one to the cliff is a wet fish!'

'Wait,' called Holly. 'I want to take a look at the chapel first.'

The chapel was a grey-stone gothic building with a green leaded roof and small carved gargoyles round the guttering. Its arched windows depicted various Biblical scenes in stained glass. Holly approached the heavy wooden door. She took hold of the round iron loop that formed the handle and gave it a twist. The door remained firmly closed.

'You won't get in there without a key,' said a man's voice. The three girls looked round.

A tall, middle-aged man with a lined weather-beaten face and a tangle of wild grey hair was walking towards them from the side of the house. He was wearing paint-spattered overalls and a broad grin.

'You'll be the three girls Susan mentioned,' he said. 'My name's Tom Catchpole. Is Susan about at all?'

'She said she had some phone-calls to make,' said Belinda.

'Oh, right,' said Tom. 'I'd better leave it for a bit.

It was nothing terribly important. I just wanted a word about setting up the fireworks on Saturday. I need to know how much timber she'll be needing for the frames.'

'Sorry,' said Belinda. 'Can't help you there.'

'Did you want to take a look in the chapel?' asked Tom. 'I've got a key.' He pulled a long black key out of his overalls. He grinned at them. 'You're probably wondering why some scruffy workman should have a key to the Fanshaws' private chapel,' he said as he inserted the key into the lock.

'No, we didn't think that at all,' said Holly, feeling a little embarassed.

The old door swung slowly open but before the girls could make a move a loud beeping filled the air. Tom nipped in over the threshold and punched some numbers into a small control panel set on the wall by the door.

The beeping stopped.

'It's an alarm system,' he said. 'Come on in, it's perfectly OK now. John got me to rig up the system just in case anyone took a fancy to the Lady of Wrath.'

'Oh,' said Belinda. 'You're with a security firm, are you?'

'Not exactly,' said Tom. 'Jack of all trades, that's me. I do a lot of work for the Fanshaws. A bit of carpentry, a bit of making-and-mending about the house. I set up this alarm system for them and –' he paused dramatically as the girls filed into the cool of the small chapel, 'I made that!'

He pointed to a large wooden cross set above a plain stone altar at the far end of the chapel. Behind the altar hung a threadbare tapestry that still showed the pale remains of a scene with Jesus blessing a large group of children. In front of the altar stood a row of narrow pews.

'Oh!' said Holly, walking along the aisle between the pews to take a closer look at the cross. 'It's lovely.' The cross was nearly two metres tall on a black metal stand. But it wasn't made simply by fixing two lengths of wood together; Holly could see that straight away. The beams of the cross were made from skilfully jointed slats, fitted together like boxwork.

'My father is a carpenter,' Holly said, looking round at Tom. 'These sort of joints are really difficult, aren't they?'

Tom's face took on a modest expression. 'It takes a while to master the techniques,' he said. 'I just wish my son had the patience to learn the craft.'

Belinda gave a little shiver in the unexpected cool of the stone building. She looked away from the altar and her eyes widened.

'Is that Sir Brandon's tomb?' At the opposite end of the chapel stood a white stone plinth upon which lay the carved stone shape of a sleeping knight and a sleeping woman.

'It is,' said Tom. 'Those are Sir Brandon and Lady Eleanor.'

They approached the sepulchre. The recumbent statues were perfectly detailed. Sir Brandon wore a round helmet. His face was gaunt and deep-eyed with proud moustaches and a full beard. He wore chain mail and a breastplate, his hands raised on to his chest where his carved fingers held the hilt of a shining silver sword. Not a stone-carved sword, but a real, metal sword with a mass of jewels set into the hilt. The point of the sword reached Sir Brandon's feet.

'The sword is the Lady of Wrath,' said Tom. 'And that's why this place is rigged up with alarms. Those jewels are worth a fair few thousand pounds, I can tell you.'

Holly stared at the beautiful sword. From the ruby set at the top of the hilt to the point of the blade the sword was only a few centimetres shorter than she was tall. And the ornamentation was not confined to the hilt: the blade itself was covered in fine patterns chased into the steel.

Next to Sir Brandon, Lady Eleanor lay in a long

gown, a pointed hat on her head and flowing, wonderfully carved hair lying on her shoulders. She also had her hands lifted over her chest, her palms pressed together as though in prayer.

'I hope your alarm system works,' said Tracy, gazing at the sword. 'I bet there are plenty of people who'd like to get their hands on *that*!'

'Don't worry,' said Tom. 'No one can get in or out of that door without setting off the alarm. And there are only three people in the world who know the code. Me, Susan and John.'

I think you're wrong there, Holly said to herself, *I can think of at least one other person who knows the code*.

'I suppose the alarm is on every night?' Holly asked Tom.

'All day and all night while the Lady is in here,' said Tom. 'That's the only way the museum will let us have it.'

'So it would have been on last night?' said Belinda.

'Correct,' said Tom. The three girls looked at one another. If Tom was right, then Lucy must have disabled the alarm system in order to let her boyfriend in. This definitely called for another discussion.

'Has anyone told you the story behind the Lady of Wrath?' asked Tom.

'We know Sir Brandon used it to frighten off the Parliamentarian army,' said Belinda. 'Susan told us all about it last night.'

'I didn't mean that,' said Tom. 'I meant the story of the sword itself.'

'Oh,' said Tracy. 'Do you know why it's got such a strange name?'

'There's nothing strange about it once you know the legend,' said Tom. He turned to face the three girls, his voice lowering as he began to speak. 'The sword was found by Sir Brandon when he was just a boy. It seems that one day, when he was about ten years old, he was playing down by the river. His parents didn't realise that there was anything strange going on until young Brandon came running back up to the house, dragging a huge sword along behind him.'

Tom turned his head to look at the sword that lay along Sir Brandon's statue. 'This very sword.'

'Where did he get it?' asked Holly.

'That's the strangest part of this whole story,' said Tom. 'Because young Brandon Wylde insisted that the sword had been given to him by a lady who had risen up out of the waters of the River Wrath. According to Brandon the woman was dressed all in green with golden hair. She came up out of the river and placed the hilt of the sword in his hand. 'Guard this sword well,' she told him, 'for it will save you in time of great peril. And should the sword ever be taken unwilling from your hand I shall return to replace it.' And then, according to the boy, the lady simply slipped beneath the water and disappeared.' Tom gave a rolling laugh, startling the girls. 'So you can see why it's valued so highly. Not everyone is given a sword by a water-nymph.'

'But it can't really have come from the river,' said Tracy. 'I mean, that's just a fairy story, isn't it?'

'Who knows?' said Tom with a broad grin. 'All I can tell you for sure is that this sword has been known as the Lady of Wrath for the past three hundred years.' He winked at Tracy. 'And it must be called that for some reason, eh?'

They came out into the bright light and warmth of the sun. Tom pressed some buttons on the alarm control panel. The loud bleeping sounded again until he had closed and locked the door.

'There you are,' he said, pocketing the key. 'All perfectly safe and sound. Now, I'd better go and see if Susan is off the phone yet.' He waved back to them as he walked towards the house. 'See you around.'

'That was some story,' said Tracy. 'This place is just crammed solid with legends and fairy tales. I'm surprised they haven't got a ghost to top it off.'

'Who says they haven't?' said Belinda. 'Maybe it was a couple of ghosts that Holly saw last night.'

'Never,' said Holly. 'Who ever heard of a ghost using a torch? That was definitely Lucy and her boyfriend.'

'Which means she knows the code to turn the alarm off.' said Belinda. 'I wonder if Susan and John know that?'

Holly nodded. 'I was thinking the same thing,' she said grimly. 'I think it's time we had a word with Lucy Fanshaw. Some thief could come and steal that sword while she's messing around letting her boyfriend in there.'

'And what if she tells us to get lost?' asked Tracy.

'Then I'm not sure we can be expected to keep her secret any longer,' said Holly. 'Come on, you two. Let's go and find her right now.'

'Oh, dear,' sighed Belinda. 'If the way she behaved last night is anything to go by, this is not going to be any fun.'

With another heavy sigh Belinda gathered herself and followed Holly and Tracy towards the house to confront Lucy Fanshaw.

4 A midnight vanishing

'I think you should talk to Lucy,' Holly said, looking at Belinda. 'You know her better than we do.'

'You'll be lucky!' retorted Belinda. 'You saw her letting her boyfriend into the chapel; you can go and talk to her.'

'That's if it was her boyfriend,' added Tracy.

The three girls had tracked Lucy Fanshaw down to a long, luxurious ground-floor room in the south wing where she was draped over an antique couch reading a magazine and drinking a mug of coffee. The members of the Mystery Club lurked in the doorway, able to see her long pale hair over the back of the couch, but unseen themselves while they debated what to do next.

'Of course it was her boyfriend,' said Holly. 'Who else could it have been?'

'The ghost of Wylde House,' intoned Belinda. 'Maybe he's put Lucy under an evil spell. That would explain her behaviour.'

'Look, why don't we all go and talk to her?' suggested Tracy. 'There's safety in numbers.'

'I'm not scared of her,' said Holly. 'I just want to do this as tactfully as possible. It won't help if we all march in and accuse her of all sorts of things.'

'You want tact?' said Tracy. 'Well, why didn't you say so?' She stepped out from behind the doorway and marched into the long room.

'Tracy!' hissed Holly, but Tracy gave her a dismissive wave of her hand.

'Hi, Lucy,' said Tracy, leaning over the back of the couch. 'How's things?'

Belinda and Holly watched anxiously from the edge of the door. Tracy was usually about as tactful as a bull in a china shop.

'Fine, thank you,' said Lucy, looking up at Tracy with a slightly puzzled expression on her face. 'How are you enjoying your stay here?'

'It's been really interesting so far,' said Tracy. 'We think we've seen a ghost!'

Lucy stared at her and then grinned. 'Lucky you,' she said. 'I've lived here all my life and I've never seen one.' She gave Tracy a slightly patronising look. 'You are kidding me, aren't you?'

'Not at all,' Tracy said earnestly. 'In fact Holly saw two ghosts. Last night. They were out in the grounds under her bedroom window.' Tracy looked hard into Lucy's bright blue eyes. 'A ghost man and a ghost woman. And the ghost woman let the ghost man into the chapel. Isn't that amazing?'

Lucy's eyes became guarded and her smile seemed to freeze on her face.

'Do you think Susan would be interested in hearing about the ghosts, Lucy?' said Tracy. 'Holly was wondering whether we ought to tell her. I mean, ghosts are pretty interesting, aren't they? What do you think?'

'Some ghosts can be extremely nasty if they're disturbed,' Lucy said coldly. 'I'd be very careful about it if I were you.'

'Hmm, maybe,' Tracy said coolly. 'But I think we'll keep a look out for the ghosts from now on.' She gave Lucy a big innocent smile. 'If we see them again, I think we'll have to tell Susan. Anyway, it's been nice talking with you. See you around.'

Holly and Belinda ducked back as Tracy came strolling out through the doorway.

The three of them ran far enough to be out of Lucy's hearing.

Belinda put her hand on Tracy's shoulder. 'Tracy,' she said admiringly, 'I take back everything I've ever said about you. That was the most brilliant thing I've ever heard.'

'It was pretty smart, wasn't it?' said Tracy. 'Anyway, it should stop Lucy sneaking her boyfriend in here late at night now she knows we know about it.' She grinned at Holly. 'And the beauty of it is that we don't actually have to keep watch at all, so long as Lucy thinks we might be. Which means we're free now to do some real exploring.' Tracy stopped suddenly and gave Belinda a very expressive look. 'What do you mean, you take back everything you ever said about me?'

'Oh, nothing,' Belinda said airily. 'Forget I mentioned it.'

'I just hope we haven't made an enemy of Lucy,' said Holly.

'Big deal if we have!' said Belinda. 'We probably won't see much of her anyway. OK, what's the plan? Do we explore the house or the grounds?'

'The house!' said Holly. 'I want to find the priest's hole.'

'But it's such a lovely day,' said Tracy. 'I don't want to be cooped up indoors in this weather.'

'What if we have a root around in the house this morning, and then go for a stroll along the cliffs after lunch?' suggested Belinda.

'And maybe we could go and explore the old watch tower?' said Tracy.

'OK,' said Holly. 'That's settled, then. We spend

the morning in the house and the afternoon outdoors. So? Where shall we start? Top or bottom?'

They decided to start at the top of the house. A long, dusty stairway led them to a cobwebby door which seemed to be under the very arch of the roof. One fruitless wrestle with the door handle sent the three of them marching back down the stairs. The door was locked.

'The secret room wouldn't be in the attic, anyway,' reasoned Holly. 'That'd be the first place anyone would look for someone in hiding.'

'You're probably right,' said Belinda. 'If there's a secret entrance, it's going to be somewhere really ordinary. You know, the last place anyone would look.'

'OK,' said Tracy. 'Let's decide where the last place is that we'd look, and then look there first!'

'Are you sure it works like that?' said Holly. 'I mean, if we pick the last place and look there first, doesn't that make it the first place?'

Belinda laughed. 'And that would mean that the first place we intended to look would become the last place, so we ought to look there first.'

'Wait, wait!' said Tracy, holding her hands up. 'Run that past me again? Are we going to look in the last place first and the first place last, or the other way around?'

'Let's just look, shall we?' said Holly. They were in an oak-lined upper hallway. 'Now, if I remember correctly, one of the Juliana Moon mysteries involved a secret passageway. And she found it by tapping on the walls and listening for a hollow sound.'

Juliana Moon was the heroine of several mystery novels by Holly's favourite author, P.J. Benson.

The three girls spent much of the morning wandering about the house, rapping on wooden panels and plaster walls until their knuckles were sore.

'I'm getting tired of this,' said Belinda, sucking at knuckles which she'd grazed on a stretch of wall in a long room in which stood several suits of armour. From the walls of the room hung a great many old weapons. 'Isn't it lunch-time yet?'

Holly looked at her watch and was surprised to see that several hours had gone by. So far as they could tell, they had searched every stretch of hallway and corridor of the house, as well as several of the open rooms. Even Holly wasn't so wrapped up in their search to go into obviously private rooms, but nearly every available wall had been tapped, and virtually every piece of carved wood or stone or marble had been pulled at and twisted in the hope of springing a hidden catch and causing a secret panel to creak open.

'Ah, here you all are,' said Susan. 'I was wondering where you'd got to.' She came walking across the bare wooden floor, her heels clicking loudly in the echoey room. 'This is the armoury, in case you hadn't guessed.'

They followed her eyes up to the ivory-coloured wall above the huge stone chimney breast. There was a fan-shaped pattern of very long black swords as a centre-piece, surrounded by smaller swords and shields and rings of dark iron knives. On either side were displayed parallel rows of spears and pikes and a few ancient-looking muskets.

'Some of these weapons date back to the fifteenth century,' said Susan. 'The family that took over the house after the Restoration were great collectors of military paraphernalia. And those muskets on the wall over there date back to the time of the French Revolution.'

'It's almost like a museum,' said Holly, gazing up at the collection. 'Have you ever thought of opening for the public?'

'We did at one time,' said Susan. 'But we couldn't get planning permission without spending an absolute fortune making the house safe for tourists.'

'You don't mean the house is falling down?' said Tracy, looking nervously at the high ceiling.

'No,' laughed Susan. 'But the rules for a place

that opens to the public are very strict, and we just don't have that sort of money.' She smiled. 'We're not exactly poor, but we don't have a couple of hundred thousand pounds lying around either.'

'It would really cost that much?' said Belinda.

'I'm afraid so,' said Susan. 'Now, I've made a salad and there's ham and egg pie in the kitchen for anyone who feels a bit peckish. Any takers?'

Susan didn't need to make the offer twice. Lucy was nowhere to be seen, but Susan had prepared a tableful of food for the girls. While they ate, they told Susan about all the exploring they had been doing.

'I think it'll be rather better hidden that that,' said Susan. 'Hollow-sounding walls would have been a dead giveaway to the King's men. They weren't dim in those days, you know.'

'Maybe it's under a floor?' suggested Holly.

'There wouldn't be the space in the upper rooms,' said Susan, 'and the cellar floors are solid stone.'

'Has anyone counted the number of windows there are and divided them by the number of rooms?' asked Belinda. 'That way you could tell if there was a window left over. And if there was one more window than could be accounted for, you'd know it belonged to the secret room.'

'That's a nice idea,' said Susan, 'but I'm afraid

there aren't any mysterious windows, and as far as I know there aren't any rooms that are shorter than they should be to make space for a secret compartment. You're very welcome to spend all week searching if you think you'd enjoy it, but I'm fairly certain there isn't a secret room in this house.'

'Maybe we'll give it a rest for today,' Holly said reluctantly.

'Good,' said Tracy. 'Does that mean we can get out in the fresh air this afternoon?'

Belinda looked at Susan. 'We were thinking of taking a look at the watch tower,' she said. 'It is safe to go over there, isn't it?'

'Perfectly safe at low tide,' said Susan, 'so long as you stick to the sandbanks. But don't try wading through the lower places, there's a lot of very soft, squishy sand there. You might find your shoes get sucked off and are never seen again.'

The three girls took a gentle post-lunch stroll in the grounds, heading towards the tall cliffs that made a sudden end to the land.

Tracy fearlessly edged right to the grassy lip and stared down into the gulf of air. It was a good twenty-metre drop to the rocky feet of the cliffs. The gentle roll of surf was some way from the cliff foot. An undulating landscape of brown sand stretched several hundred metres out to where the white-hemmed sea lapped the shore. Over to their left, the craggy hump of land on which the ruined watch tower stood was clear of the sea, a few pools and lengths of shining water showing the places where the seabed sank to the mushy quicksands of which Susan had spoken.

'Don't go too near the edge!' yelled Belinda. 'I don't want to have to go down there and scrape you up with a spatula. What would we tell your mum?'

'Don't be silly,' said Tracy. 'I'm not going to fall. I was just seeing if there was a path down to the beach this way.'

'A path down the cliff?' said Belinda. 'I'm not risking that. What do you think I am, a monkey?'

Tracy laughed. 'Do you really want me to answer that?'

'*Is* there a way down?' asked Holly, coming as close to the edge as she dared. She wasn't as nervous of heights as Belinda, but the way the cliff just fell sheer away beneath her made her feel a little giddy.

'Nope,' Tracy said disappointedly, 'it doesn't look like it. I guess we'll have to go all the way back to the house and down to the causeway. It looks like that's the only way to get out there.'

'Look,' said Belinda, who was feeling the effects of rather too much lunch. 'The watch tower will still be there tomorrow. What say we just mooch around up here today?' She gazed out over the sea. 'It's such a lovely view from here.'

'OK,' said Tracy. 'I guess it'd be nice to just sit here and soak up some sun.' She eyed Belinda. 'Especially those of us who had three helpings of pie.'

'I only ate it to be polite,' Belinda said with dignity. 'After all that trouble Susan had gone to, it seemed a shame to let it go to waste.' She walked through the rough grass. 'And if you're suggesting that I eat too much, then all I can say to you is – *whoops!*' She lurched as her foot caught on the edge of a half-hidden hole in the ground. She windmilled her arms and regained her balance. 'What a stupid place to leave a hole!' she said. 'I could have broken my leg!'

'There's another one over here,' said Holly. She crouched down. Under a cap of waving grass the cleft seemed to go down a long way into the hillside. 'What do you think they are?'

'Who knows?' said Tracy. 'Landslips, maybe? You know, where the cliff is beginning to fall apart?'

'Oh, thanks!' said Belinda. 'That's a great comfort. Well, that settles it, I'm getting right away from the edge.'

They finally found a place to Belinda's liking and the three friends spent the rest of the afternoon contentedly watching the seagulls and chatting about where the secret room could be.

It was astonishing, but for the second night running, the three girls found themselves yawning in their chairs only a short time after dinner. Belinda and Susan were playing backgammon and Tracy and Holly were looking at a large old atlas that Susan had brought from the library. The maps inside dated from the seventeenth and eighteenth century and were absolutely fascinating.

But even that couldn't prevent Holly from wanting her bed by mid-evening.

'I feel like I could sleep for twenty-four hours,' she said to her friends.

'Good,' said Belinda. 'Then you won't be dragging me out of bed at the crack of dawn like you did today.'

'The crack of dawn!' said Tracy. 'It was nine o'clock.'

'That's the same thing when I'm on holiday,'

grinned Belinda. 'See you in the morning. *Late* in the morning.'

Holly was wrong about one thing. She didn't sleep for twenty-four hours, or anything like it. In fact she woke up in the dark for the second time in a row. She fumbled for her watch and read the luminous dial. It was just past midnight. She'd only been asleep for two hours!

She tried to get back off to sleep. But there was a problem. A very annoying problem. She was thirsty. The nearest source of water was the bathroom at the end of the corridor. But was she thirsty enough to bother going there?

After ten minutes of tossing and turning she decided she was. She put on her dressing-gown and crept across the floor. Her door creaked as she opened it. A pale, ghostly light filtered through the long windows, giving enough illumination to allow her to negotiate her way along the corridor.

A small sound startled her and she stopped, her heart beating curiously loud in her ears.

It's a good thing I don't believe in ghosts, she said to herself. *Because this is exactly the sort of house I'd be in if I was a ghost*!

She heard the sound again. The crisp click of a lock either opening or closing, followed by soft footfalls. Someone else was up and about in the dark of midnight. Someone who was moving stealthily along the corridor just around the bend where the bathroom was situated.

It couldn't be Tracy or Belinda, Holly reasoned. The doors to their rooms were in plain sight. So it had to be either Susan or Lucy. Unless . . . unless it was an intruder. The young man Lucy had let into the chapel? Maybe tonight she had brought him into the house.

Hardly breathing, Holly slid along the corridor and risked a glance round the corner. Lucy Fanshaw was walking away from her towards the main staircase, her long hair shining eerily in the moonlight. And she wasn't wearing a dressing-gown, as Holly would have expected in the middle of the night. She was dressed in a black sweater and black jeans.

Lucy moved out of sight and Holly followed, tiptoeing in the mysterious girl's silent wake, ready to duck out of sight the moment Lucy appeared again.

Holly came to the end of the corridor and looked down into the well of the main hall. Lucy had descended the stairs and was gliding towards the left – towards the north wing.

The moment she was out of sight, Holly went

creeping down the stairs, determined to discover what Lucy was up to.

It was strange. There was no way out of the house from the north wing, unless Lucy was intending to crawl out through a window. So what was she doing?

Holly stood perfectly still at the foot of the stairs and listened. She could hear footsteps. She followed, her own feet bare and consequently almost silent. Lucy's steps took on a hollow, echoey sound. Holly recognised it. It was the sound made by entering the uncarpeted and half-empty armoury.

Holly moved to the armoury door. There was a problem now. There was only one way in or out of the armoury. As soon as Lucy had done whatever she'd gone in there to do, she'd have to leave by the same entrance – and that risked her walking straight into Holly.

Holly tried to cram herself into a dark corner, hoping that Lucy wouldn't look in that direction on her way out.

There was a soft scraping noise from within the armoury and then silence. Holly licked her dry lips, wishing Belinda and Tracy were there with her.

The blood sang in her ears, but otherwise the night was completely silent. Holly began to feel cramped. There was not a single sound from the armoury. Whatever Lucy was doing there, she was doing it in total silence.

At last Holly couldn't stand it any more. She prised herself out of her hiding-place and edged her head round the open doorway. The armoury was full of silvery moonlight, throwing the square patterns of the mullioned windows out over the floor and glinting on the metalwork of the weapons that hung from the walls.

Holly's mouth fell open in surprise and her eyes grew as round as saucers.

The armoury was completely deserted. Lucy had vanished!

5 Theft!

It was impossible. But as Holly looked around the long moonlit armoury she had to accept that the impossible had happened. Lucy Fanshaw had walked into that room not five minutes previously and seemed simply to have winked out of existence.

Holly stepped into the room. There was very little in the way of furniture. A couple of antique black wooden chairs, two small black chests and one very large chest under the windows at the far end. A black chest with black metal bindings. It was large enough for someone to hide in, but Holly couldn't believe that Lucy had come in here to hide herself in a box. It didn't make any sense.

Holly padded across the floor, her eyes searching for any sign of an open window; for *anything* to reveal how Lucy had got out of the room.

She came to the large chest and tried to lift the lid. But it was locked. A sudden dry scrape sounded behind her. Instinctively, Holly dived down into the tight squeeze between the chest and the waist-high wooden wainscoting that lined the wall.

'I'm starving.' It was the voice of a young man.

'Shh!' A girl's voice. *Lucy's* voice! 'Not so loud!'

'There's no one here,' said the male voice. 'What are you so jumpy about?'

'Those three brats that my dad invited to stay,' said Lucy. 'They saw us last night. They've threatened to tell my mum if they see us again.'

'They'll regret it if they do,' said the man, whom Holly assumed to be the mysterious Colin. 'I can deal with three nosy kids.'

'What do you mean?' asked Lucy.

'I'd shut them up once and for all if they ruined this,' growled the young man.

'You won't have to,' said Lucy, her voice sounding a little anxious, as though the man's words had unnerved her. 'All we need to do is to be more careful. And keep your voice down. Those three must have seen the torchlight last night. That's why I didn't bring the torch tonight.' Her voice took on an urgency. 'When are we going to do it?'

'Not just yet,' said Colin. 'I think we should give it one more day.'

'OK,' breathed Lucy. 'I can wait a bit longer.

And then we'll show my dad whether I'm a child or not.'

The voices began to fade as the two people headed towards the armoury door.

'Have you got the paint?' asked Colin.

'Yes. It's all ready,' said Lucy. 'And once we've hidden it, my dad won't ever find it without my help.'

The last thing Holly heard was the young man complain again about being hungry, and then the voices were gone.

Holly lifted her head over the rim of the chest. There was no doubt in her mind about what had happened. It was obvious. She ran to the door, checked that Lucy and Colin were gone, and then ran as quickly and silently as she could up to the corridor where she and her two friends had their bedrooms.

Tracy was easiest to rouse. A hand on her shoulder, a murmured word in her ear and Tracy was out of the bed and ready for action. Belinda was a different proposition, but even she managed to shake the sleep out of her head as Holly recounted what she had just witnessed.

'Lucy must have gone out through some kind of secret passage,' said Holly. 'And she's brought her boyfriend into the house.'

'I thought we weren't going to get involved in this,' said Belinda, rubbing her eyes.

'But the secret passage!' said Holly. 'Don't you get it? She's found a secret passage.'

Belinda sat bolt upright in bed. 'Oh! Which means she must have found the secret room. Crumbs!'

'Holly, you're a marvel!' said Tracy. 'So, where's the secret entrance? Did you see what Lucy did to get it open?'

'No, I was hiding,' said Holly. 'But it's in the armoury, I know that much. And there's more. I think they've got some plan to get back at John.'

'What do you mean?' asked Tracy. 'What sort of plan?'

'I'm not sure,' said Holly. She told her friends what she had heard Colin and Lucy say.

'It sounds like they're planning to steal something,' said Belinda. 'Or to hide something, to give John a scare.'

'You do realise where the secret passage must lead to, don't you?' said Holly. 'It explains why the light just disappeared in the chapel last night. They didn't go into another room in there. There *isn't* another room in the chapel. They must have gone into a passageway that leads from the chapel to the armoury.'

'Hey,' said Tracy, 'if they've found the priest's

hole, maybe they've found the treasure, too. Maybe that's what they were talking about. They're going to steal the treasure.'

'But what are we going to do about it?' asked Belinda. 'Tell Susan?'

'We need to be sure first,' said Holly. 'I heard Colin say that they wouldn't be doing whatever they're planning on doing for another day, so we've got all of tomorrow to try and work out what they're up to.'

'And if we can't?' asked Belinda.

'Then we tell Susan everything we know,' said Holly. 'I don't like the idea of telling on Lucy, but I don't see what other choice we've got.'

Even Belinda was up reasonably early the following morning. Susan and the three girls were eating breakfast at the kitchen table when Lucy came strolling in.

'Hello, darling,' said Susan. 'What plans have you got for today?'

'Nothing at all!' snapped Lucy. She scraped marmalade on a slice of toast, poured a cup of coffee and walked out of the kitchen without even acknowledging the existence of the three houseguests.

'Take no notice of her,' said Susan as brightly

as she could. 'She's still upset about her boyfriend going away.'

That's what you think, thought Holly.

After breakfast they had a quick Mystery Club meeting out on the sun-drenched lawn.

'OK,' said Holly, 'we've got plenty of work on today.' She took out the Mystery Club's red notebook and started to write. 'I've been thinking,' she said. 'Lucy and Colin are planning on taking something and hiding it to pay her father back for having Colin sent to Manchester. That's what I think.'

'Excuse me,' said Tracy. 'If you're right, Colin hasn't gone to Manchester.'

'Of course he hasn't,' said Holly. 'But everyone except Lucy thinks he has. The way I see it, Colin's father sent him away, just like Lucy said. But Colin didn't go. He's been hiding here ever since.'

'Why do you think that?' asked Tracy.

'That's easy,' said Belinda. 'Colin was starving, he said, so he can't have been at home. Holly's right. He's been lurking around here, and Lucy's been feeding him. That's what the midnight visits have been all about. The question now is: what are they planning on stealing and hiding?'

'I told you that last night,' said Tracy. 'Lady Eleanor's treasure! It must be!'

Holly shook her head. 'I don't see how, Tracy. That doesn't fit in with what they were saying. Why would they talk about hiding the treasure to teach John a lesson? John doesn't even know the treasure exists, does he?'

'The Lady of Wrath!' exclaimed Belinda. 'That's what they've got planned. They're going to steal the Lady of Wrath.'

'I think you're right,' Holly said, writing this down in the notebook. 'I think they're going to hide it, and Lucy's going to refuse to say where it is unless John allows her to carry on seeing Colin. I'll bet it's something like that.'

'Huh!' said Tracy. 'I know how my dad would react if I ever tried something like that on him!' Tracy's American father had stayed in California after the divorce when Tracy and her English mother had come to live in Willow Dale three years earlier.

'Mine too,' said Holly. 'But Lucy is obviously totally spoilt. And she might think her father would cave in to her.'

'OK,' said Belinda. 'Let's say we're right, and the pair of them intend to sneak off with the Lady of Wrath. Now, if the sword goes missing, we can go to Susan and tell her that we know what's happened. Or we can stop it happening in the first place.'

'Like, how?' asked Tracy. 'Tell Lucy we've sussed her out?'

'As a last resort,' said Belinda. 'But supposing we were to find the secret passage today? We know what room it's in now, so it's just a case of having a thorough search.' She grinned. 'And then, of course, we go straight off to tell Susan. And then everyone knows about the passage, which means Lucy and her pal wouldn't dare to carry on using it. And there you are! Prevention rather than cure! We stop them stealing the sword in the first place, as easy as that!'

'So it's everyone into the armoury, right?' said Tracy. 'And we take the place apart until we find the secret entrance.'

'I think one of us should keep an eye on Lucy,' said Holly.

'And one of us should keep another eye open for any sign of Colin,' said Belinda. 'I think we should split up, at least for a few hours. One to find Lucy and follow her. One to scout around out here and see if they can find where Colin's been hiding, and one to have a thorough search of the armoury.'

'So who does what?' asked Tracy.

Holly plucked up three blades of grass and tore them to different lengths. 'The longest is the armoury, the middle is Colin and the short one is Lucy,' she said, putting the blades of grass in her fist so it was impossible to tell which was which.

Belinda picked the armoury blade and Tracy picked the one for following Lucy.

'Which leaves me to search out here,' said Holly. 'And we all meet up again around lunch-time to compare notes. Unless something important happens before then, in which case it's up to the one who's discovered something to find the others. OK?'

'OK,' Tracy said to Holly. 'I guess it was a fair draw, even though you get to stroll around out here and Belinda has all the fun of looking for the secret passage while I've got to find that horrible girl and follow her around all morning.'

'If it makes you feel any better,' Belinda said with a smile, 'I promise not to enjoy myself too much.'

Holly tucked her notebook into the back pocket of her jeans as Belinda and Tracy headed for the house.

It certainly was another lovely day. Beyond the distant grassy lip of the cliff the sea sparkled in the sunlight.

Now then, thought Holly, as she scanned the long curve of the hill. *Where would a good hiding-place be?* There was nowhere obvious near the house. The chapel was the only other building. There were trees in the distance. Holly imagined that a person could camp out in the woods quite easily in all the warm weather they were having.

She took another look at the chapel. A thought had struck her. Lucy had clearly discovered some way of deactivating the alarm system. Once she had let Colin into the chapel, why should he hide anywhere else? Especially as the passage must lead to the priest's hole. He could hide in there all day, and come out at night for food.

Holly did feel one twinge of disappointment in all this. If their theory was correct, then it was virtually certain that there was no hidden treasure in the secret room. It wasn't believable that Lucy could have found a room full of lost treasures without telling anyone.

Holly walked over to the chapel and stood on tiptoe to peer in through a stained glass window. She could see the rows of pews and the stone altar with the tall wooden cross behind it. She angled her head and looked down the chapel to the tomb of Sir Brandon and Lady Eleanor. The Lady of Wrath glinted in the coloured light that poured through the windows. At least the sword hadn't been taken yet.

'Hello, hello,' called a cheerful voice. 'Isn't it a fabulous day? Let's hope it keeps up for the weekend.'

Holly looked round. Tom Catchpole was striding across the grass towards the chapel.

'Hello,' said Holly. 'Are you looking for Susan?'

'Not really,' said Tom. 'I've just delivered the timber for the firework frames. I thought I'd just check that the alarm is working.' He grinned. 'We don't want the Lady of Wrath to go walkies, do we?'

Holly followed him around to the side of the chapel.

'Where are your friends?' he asked as he felt in his overalls pockets for the key to the chapel door.

'Oh, they're around somewhere,' said Holly. 'In fact, I was just off to find them.' At least, Holly had decided to go and speak to Belinda. Her new idea about Colin's likely hiding-place meant that there was no point in her wandering about outside. She could help with the search for the secret passage.

Tom opened the chapel and stepped smartly over the threshold as the alarm gave out its warning beep.

'See you later,' Holly called as she headed towards the house.

'Sure thing,' said Tom as he closed the chapel door behind him. A second later the beeping stopped.

I wonder what he'd think if he knew that even someone like Lucy can cut the alarm off? Holly said to herself. *But I suppose it can't be too difficult from the inside, if you know the code.*

Holly was about to enter the house through the back door that led to the kitchen when she heard a shout. She spun around in time to see Tom come running out of the chapel with an expression of pure panic on his face.

She ran towards him. 'What's wrong?' she gasped. 'What's happened?'

'I've got to call the police,' he panted as he charged past her towards the back door. 'The sword! It's the sword! It's been stolen!'

Holly gaped at him, hardly able to believe her ears. It wasn't possible. Not five minutes previously she had seen the sword in its usual place in Sir Brandon Wylde's hands.

Tom disappeared into the house and Holly went racing down to the open chapel door. She came to a skidding halt in the cool interior of the chapel.

The stone effigy of Sir Brandon Wylde lay as

ever upon his cold tomb, his hands lifted to his chest, fingers cupped to receive the jewelled hilt of the Lady of Wrath.

But the sword which had lain there glinting in the coloured light only a few minutes previously was gone.

Holly let out a groan of despair. Somehow in those few minutes it seemed that Lucy and Colin had struck. The Lady of Wrath was gone, despite everything the Mystery Club had tried to do to prevent it.

6 A confrontation

Belinda and Tracy split up in the main hall of the house. Belinda headed off towards the armoury while Tracy made for the long room in the south wing where they had found Lucy the previous day.

Lucy wasn't in the first room where Tracy looked. The problem was that as they hadn't seen her since her brief ill-tempered appearance at breakfast, Tracy couldn't even be sure that the young woman was still at home.

She went to the front of the house and looked through a window. Lucy's sports car was still parked in the drive.

Good, thought Tracy, *That means she's got to be around here somewhere*.

Susan was in a room with a large desk covered in papers and documents. She was busy on the telephone, and judging by what she was saying she was deep in preparations for Saturday's big event.

Tracy crept away so as not to disturb her and headed upstairs. She had a fairly good idea of where Lucy's room was. She passed their own bedrooms and turned the corner of the corridor where the bathroom was situated. There were four doors in this stretch of corridor, and one of them belonged to Lucy's room.

Tracy listened at one. Nothing. She moved to the next and pressed her ear to the panels.

'Can I help you?'

Tracy nearly jumped clean out of her shoes. Lucy was standing right behind her as if she had just materialised out of thin air.

'I was looking for . . . for the . . . uh . . . bathroom,' stammered Tracy.

Lucy smiled a thin little smile. 'I think you'll find it back there,' she said, hooking a thumb over her shoulder. 'Where it's always been. You'll know it when you see it; it's the room with the enamel plaque screwed to the door. The plaque that says "bathroom".'

Tracy shot Lucy her most innocent and disarming smile.

'It sure is easy to get lost in this house,' she said. She walked to the bathroom and opened the door. Lucy was standing in the corridor looking at her with a very cold expression on her face.

Tracy stepped into the bathroom and closed the door. She could feel her cheeks burning with embarrassment. Lucy must have guessed what she was up to. Tracy just wished she'd been able to come up with a convincing excuse. She felt a complete fool!

She gave it a minute or two and then opened the bathroom door a crack. Lucy hadn't gone far. She was at the end of the corridor, standing with her back to Tracy as though in deep thought. And then, as Tracy watched, Lucy made a sudden dash to the right.

Tracy was out of the bathroom like an arrow. Moving almost silently, she ran after Lucy. She stopped at the corner and edged an eye around. Lucy was walking briskly along. She glanced around once but Tracy ducked her head back and was pretty sure she wasn't seen.

As soon as Lucy turned another corner, Tracy was after her. If Lucy was up to something that she didn't want known about, then Tracy was determined to find out what.

Hey, she thought, *maybe she's got that boy hidden in the house somewhere! Maybe she's going to see him right now*.

Spurred on by this thought, Tracy continued her silent pursuit of the elusive young woman. She suddenly realised where Lucy was headed. The three members of the Mystery Club had been this way yesterday morning. It was the corridor that led to the long stairway up to that locked door under the roof.

Tracy peered round the final corner. Lucy was nowhere to be seen, but this section of corridor led only to the stairs. She must have gone up that way. Tracy ran to the foot of the stairs. The attic door was open.

Tracy bit her bottom lip, trying to decide what she should do. Should she run down and get Belinda and Holly or should she climb the stairs to see exactly what Lucy was up to?

It only took a moment for Tracy to make her mind up. She had to go up there.

She crept up the stairs, alert for any sound. The attic room was shrouded in darkness but from the shapes that lurked in the gloom it seemed to be filled with all sorts of junk and jumble. Cautiously Tracy stepped over the threshold. She felt a draught of air at her back as the door slammed behind her. There was the clack of a key turning, a soft female laugh and the sound of feet descending the stairs.

'Hey!' shouted Tracy, hammering on the door with both fists. 'Hey! Let me out of here!'

* * *

Now then, Belinda thought to herself as she stood in the wide doorway of the armoury. *Where's the most likely place for someone to put a secret entrance?*

The room was at the corner of the house, both its long left-hand wall and the shorter end wall being comprised mostly of tall narrow windows. Belinda began a tour of the room. Certainly the outer walls of the house were thick, but she doubted that they were thick enough to contain a secret passage. No, the entrance had to be in the other long wall; the wall with the massive fireplace and chimney breast. From chest height up the wall was smooth ivory-coloured plaster, but below that was the wooden-panelled wainscoting.

The three of them had already been in that room, tapping at the wooden panels in the hope of hearing the hollow sound that would reveal the hidden entrance.

Belinda went slowly along the wall, rapping with her knuckles again and listening carefully. But it was just the same as it had been the previous morning. If one of these panels covered a hole, then it wasn't going to be found by tapping.

Belinda walked the length of the wall a second time, testing the panels and their surrounds for any hint of movement.

And then a thought struck her. She ducked down and peered into the dark recesses of the great fireplace. The highest point of the stone arch was at Belinda's shoulder height, but beyond the arch the fireplace was expansive enough to fit several quite tall people within. The brickwork walls were blackened as if with years and years of soot, but as Belinda crouched and twisted her head upwards she could see that the chimney itself had been closed off at some stage by a black metal sheet that lay across the brickwork a metre above her head. The fireplace didn't seem to have been used for a long time.

She stretched her neck to look at the darkened side walls of the deep recess.

'Oh!' She stared down at the stone floor. She crept right in under the arch and crouched in the inglenook, reaching down and picking something up in her fingers.

It was a few scraps of grass and a couple of little clods of earth. The kind of stuff that would get stuck under the shoe of someone walking across a lawn. But the spears of grass were still green and the earth was still a little damp.

'Got you!' breathed Belinda. That stuff had not been there very long. There was only one explanation. The grass and earth had been scraped off the bottom of a shoe belonging either to Lucy or her boyfriend. Belinda had found the entrance to the secret passage.

She stood up and rubbed her hands on her sweat-shirt. Now there was only one more thing to do. One little thing.

Belinda stared at the blank soot-stained wall at the side of the fireplace. All she had to do was find the trigger to open the secret doorway.

Tracy Foster, you are the dumbest person in the entire world.

Tracy stared at the locked attic door. *You were totally suckered. Lucy led you here by the nose. She brought you up here and locked you in like you didn't have two brain cells to rub together!*

Tracy let out a snort of exasperation. She rattled the door handle for a few moments; more to relieve her frustration than in any hope that the door would open.

The room wasn't quite as dark as she had at first thought. There was a low gable window through which some grimy sunlight was able to filter. But her first impression of the attic room had been correct. It teemed with rubbish. Everything from a huge old wardrobe to broken chairs and rolls of dusty carpet and tea-chests filled with every sort of discarded junk you could imagine.

Tracy picked her way through the obstacle course of household debris and rubbed her sleeve against the dust-caked window. Far below her the lawns and flower-beds of Wylde House spread out to the distant woodlands and, to her left, the sparkle of the sea.

She tried the window catch and was quite surprised when it gave easily and the window came open. She leaned out. Only a metre or so below her was a level area of roofing bordered with a low brick parapet. She twisted her head to look in both directions. The flat walkway went both ways. It was narrow but the knee-high brickwork of the wall made it look reasonably safe for a person who didn't suffer from vertigo.

There didn't seem much option but to climb through the window and try to find some other way back into the house. She could yell and beat on the door in the hope of someone coming close enough to hear her, but in such a big house she could yell for *hours* without being heard. No, the window was the best bet. And once she'd found a way down again, she'd have a few sharp words to say to Lucy Fanshaw!

A cool wind ruffled Tracy's blonde hair as she

stepped out on to the roof. The attic window was one of several that punched up in gables through the slate roof. She edged along to the next one but she wasn't able to get it open. She was just wondering whether her best bet would be to yell for help over the edge of the raised wall when she spotted a skylight.

It lay on the slope of the roof, about two metres up. Tracy carefully tested the slates, not entirely sure that they would support her weight. But they seemed solid enough as she leaned forward and scrambled up to grab hold of the frame of the skylight.

She levered herself up with her feet. Through the skylight she could see a small room with angled walls. There was an old bath against one wall, and a sort of cabinet, but otherwise the little room was empty.

Tracy drew herself up on to her knees, slipping a little on the slope, but managing not to slide down. She dug her fingers in under the frame and heaved. Her feet slid away from under her on the slates and she gave a cry of alarm as she found herself tobogganing down to the narrow walkway. A single, precarious row of bricks was all that stood between her and a terrible fall.

Her feet struck up against the low wall. Tracy

felt a small, alarming movement in the brickwork and a few pieces of mortar fall away. But the wall held and, after taking a few deep, calming breaths, Tracy crawled back up to the skylight.

Making sure that her foothold was as secure as possible, Tracy again took hold of the frame of the skylight. She pulled upwards. There was a brittle crack as the weather-rotten wood gave under her fingers and the skylight creaked and groaned open.

It was heavier than she had expected and it took all her strength to raise it enough for her to bring her legs round and slide them over the edge into the room. She wriggled round on to her stomach, fending the skylight off with one arm as she wormed downwards and made the last short jump to the bare floorboards. The skylight closed with a thump.

The door of the small unused bathroom was open. It led to another empty room from which led several doors and a dusty, uncarpeted stairway.

Brushing the dust and grime off her clothes, Tracy ran down the stairs to a brown door. It opened and led her back into the main part of the house.

OK, Miss Lucy Smartypants, Tracy thought determinedly. *I'm going to find you and even things up between us!*

* * *

Holly raced out of the chapel, her mind in a whirl. Their suspicions simply had to be correct. Lucy's secret passage led from the armoury to the chapel, and in those few minutes between Holly seeing the sword through the chapel window and Tom letting himself in, Lucy and Colin must have used the passage to steal the sword.

Holly turned right as she entered the house and ran down the long corridor to the armoury. Her fear was that Belinda might have disturbed the two thieves on their way out of the passage with the sword; she could be in serious trouble.

But the armoury was deserted. Holly came to a panting halt in the middle of the floor.

'Where is she?' she gasped.

'Whoo-oo-oo! This is the ghost of Eleanor Wylde come to haunt you! Whoo-oo!'

Holly spun round at Belinda's voice.

'Where are you?' she shouted.

Belinda's head popped out from under the arch of the fireplace. 'Coo-ee!'

'The sword's been stolen!' yelled Holly.

'What?' gasped Belinda. 'When?'

'About five minutes ago!' said Holly. 'One minute it was there, and the next it was gone! It had to be Lucy and Colin; they must have used the passage to get into the chapel. There's no other way they could have got in there.'

'They didn't come this way,' said Belinda. 'I've been here all the time. And I know exactly where the passage comes out.' She beckoned to Holly. 'Come here, I'll show you.'

Holly ducked under the arch of the fireplace and Belinda showed her where she had found the grass and earth scrapings.

'OK,' said Holly. 'There are only two things that can have happened. Either there's another way out of the passageway, or they're still hiding in there with the sword.'

'We've got to tell Susan,' said Belinda. 'We can't keep all this quiet now.'

'I know,' said Holly. 'Look, you stay here, just in case they come out this way. If you see anything, yell like mad and I'll come running. I'm going to find Susan.'

It didn't take Holly long to track Susan down in her study. As Holly burst in, Susan was just putting the telephone down after having spoken to the police. Tom Catchpole was standing by the desk.

'It's all my fault,' he was saying. 'Susan, how can I apologise? I was sure that security system was foolproof, but someone must have found a way to break the circuit. They must have done it last night. I'm so sorry!'

'No!' exclaimed Holly. 'You're wrong! The sword was there only a few minutes ago. I saw it! And I know how it was stolen. There's a secret passage from the armoury to the chapel.'

Susan Fanshaw stared at her. 'Holly? What on earth are you talking about?'

'We've found the secret passage!' Holly blurted. But then she faltered. How could she explain to Susan what Lucy and Colin had been up to in the dead of night?

'Secret passage?' said a voice from behind Holly. 'What secret passage is this?'

Holly spun around. Lucy was standing right behind her in the doorway.

Holly stared at her in amazement, but she quickly gathered her scattered wits.

'I think you should tell Susan,' she said.

Lucy's eyebrows arched. 'Tell her what? What's going on in here?'

'The Lady of Wrath has been stolen,' said Susan.

The colour drained from Lucy's face. 'What?' She seemed genuinely shocked by her mother's words.

'Don't pretend you don't know anything about it,' said Holly.

'Oh, be quiet,' spat Lucy. 'What's going on here, Mother?'

Holly was about to say something when Tracy appeared at the doorway.

'You idiot!' she shouted at Lucy. 'I could have been locked up there all day!'

'Then you should learn not to follow me about,' snapped Lucy. 'I'm sick and tired of you three brats.' She glared at her mother. 'They've been trying to get back at me ever since I forgot to pick them up at the station! Anyone would think they were six-year-olds the way they're behaving!'

'For heaven's sake!' shouted Susan. 'What on earth is everyone talking about?'

'Lucy just locked me in an attic,' said Tracy. 'Look at the state of my clothes! I had to climb out on the roof to get back inside.'

'Lucy, is this true?' asked Susan.

'Yes,' said Lucy. 'I told you, they've been following me about, and I'm sick of it. And they've been making up stupid stories about me. I've heard them! They were planning on telling you a lot of nonsense about me being in the chapel with someone. And I'm supposed to have found some secret passageway.' She folded her arms and glared at Holly. 'Go on, tell her all those ridiculous lies you were making up about me.'

'They're not lies,' Holly said softly but determinedly. 'I did see you in the chapel – and you were with Colin!'

'Colin!' The cry came from both Susan and Tom.

'If you're going to make up lies about me,' said Lucy, 'then at least try to make up believable ones.'

'What do you know about Colin, Holly?' said Susan.

'Not much,' said Holly. 'I heard him mentioned the other night. That first night, when Lucy got home.'

Susan frowned at her. 'Then you should know that Colin is in Manchester.'

'I don't think he is,' said Holly.

'I'm not going to pretend to understand a single word of this,' said Tom, looking hard at Holly. 'But I can tell you one thing for certain. My son is definitely in Manchester with his mother.'

'*Your* son?' gasped Tracy. 'Colin is *your* son?'

'That's right,' said Tom. 'And I spoke to him on the phone only this morning. He's with his mother in Manchester, I can guarantee that.'

'So?' said Lucy, staring into Holly's troubled eyes. 'Have you got any more lies to tell about me?'

Holly stared round at them all, her head in a spin. She met Tracy's eyes but saw only confusion in her friend's gaze. Suddenly even Tracy seemed uncertain, and the worst part of it was that neither Tracy nor Belinda had actually seen anything. They had both relied on Holly's word. But would the same hold true for Susan and Tom? Who would they be most likely to believe? Someone they'd known for years, or a total stranger?

'Well, Holly?' Susan's voice was very stern.

Holly swallowed. There was one last hope. The secret passage. If they could prove that the passage existed then maybe the rest of her story would be believed.

Otherwise, it was a simple case of Holly's word against Lucy's, and Holly had the dreadful feeling that Susan and Tom Catchpole were more likely to believe that Lucy was telling the truth.

7 Stalemate

Holly looked at the faces of the people around her. Susan's was grim and pale, as was Tom Catchpole's. They were waiting for her to speak. She held Tracy's eyes for a moment, knowing immediately that her friend would back her up no matter what happened. And then Holly looked into Lucy's face. What she saw in Lucy's cold look convinced her that the young woman was prepared to tell any number of lies.

It all rested on finding a way into that secret passage. But what if they couldn't? They certainly weren't going to get any help from Lucy. How would it look to Susan, thought Holly, if she persisted in her accusations and was unable to prove a thing?

Holly licked her lips and turned to look at Susan Fanshaw.

'I'm sorry,' she said, the words coming with difficulty through her dry throat. It was hard for her to apologise when she was so certain that Lucy was involved in the theft of the sword. 'I thought I saw someone in the chapel, but I must have been wrong.'

'Holly?' gasped Tracy.

Holly linked eyes with her friend, staring her into a baffled silence.

She turned to Lucy. 'I'm very sorry,' she said. 'It was late at night and I'd only just woken up. I must have imagined it.' She looked at Susan and gave a bleak smile. 'My parents are always telling me not to let my imagination run away with me, aren't they, Tracy?'

'Well, yes, but—' began Tracy.

'We really didn't mean to try and get Lucy into trouble,' said Holly, silencing her friend. 'The whole thing has been a big mistake.'

'But you said you'd found a secret passage,' said Susan.

Holly gave her a shamefaced look. 'We thought we might have done, but it probably isn't. Look, I'm really sorry. I feel terrible about this. I'll pack my case and catch the next train home if you like.'

'There's no need for that,' Susan said briskly. 'I think you've been a bit silly, Holly, and you should really be more careful of your facts before you go accusing innocent people of things. But there's no harm done. In the circumstances, I think it would be best for us all to forget about it.'

'I agree,' said Tom. 'We've got enough problems with the theft.'

'The police should be here soon,' said Susan. 'I expect they'll want to interview everyone.' She looked at Tracy and Holly. 'I think you two and Belinda should stay in the house until after the police have been. And you, Lucy, don't you go gallivanting off anywhere, either.'

'But I don't know anything about the theft,' Lucy said angrily.

'I'm sure you don't,' said Susan. 'But the police may want to speak to you anyway, so don't go anywhere, OK?'

Wordlessly, Holly turned and left the office. Tracy followed her, linking arms with her as they walked along the corridor.

'Why didn't you tell them everything about what that girl's been up to?' Tracy asked once they were out of earshot of the others. 'I'd have backed you up.'

'I know you would,' said Holly. 'Don't worry, I haven't given up altogether. Let's go and find Belinda.'

Belinda was standing at the armoury door, impatiently staring out along the corridor, desperate to find out what was going on.

'About time!' she called as her two friends appeared.

'Have you found how to get into the passageway?' asked Holly.

'No,' said Belinda. 'I've tried everything, short of attacking the wall with a pickaxe. What have you been doing? Have you told Susan about Lucy and Colin?'

'It wasn't Colin,' Tracy said gloomily.

'It wasn't?' said Belinda. 'How do you know?'

'Because Tom Catchpole is Colin's father,' said Holly. 'And he spoke to Colin on the phone in Manchester this morning.'

'Crumbs,' breathed Belinda. 'So who was Lucy with?'

'I don't know,' said Holly. 'Lucy denied everything and told Susan that we were making up stories about her.'

'It was really bad,' said Tracy. She told Belinda all that had happened in Susan's study.

'But you know they were involved,' said Belinda. 'They must have been. Didn't you tell them that you saw the sword only a couple of minutes before it vanished?'

'Yes, but they're going to think that was just me and my overactive imagination again.' Holly's face became grim. 'At least, I *hope* that's what they're going to think.'

'Why do you hope that?' asked Tracy.

'Because if everyone, including Lucy, thinks we're a lot of silly little girls,' said Holly, 'then no one's going to think we're still investigating. Look, Lucy is going to deny anything we say, right? And the only way we can prove that she and that man are involved is by finding how that secret passage opens.'

'I told you,' said Belinda. 'I've tried everything. I've prodden and poked and twisted and shoved every single brick in that fireplace. I don't think we'll ever be able to figure it out.'

'Exactly,' said Holly. 'So we need it to be opened *for* us.'

'But the only people who know how to work it are Lucy and that man,' said Tracy. Then a light went on in her head. 'Oh, I get it. One of us hides in here and keeps watch until Lucy comes in and uses the passage.'

'That's exactly what we're going to do,' said Holly. 'It nearly choked me back there, having to apologise in front of everyone. We're going to find out how that passage opens and then we're going to tell Susan, Tom and the police the whole story. And let's see Lucy worm her way out of that one!'

Things in Wylde House were very strained for the rest of the day. Holly was sure that Susan was puzzled and disappointed by her, and that hurt more than anything. But she was determined to say nothing until the Mystery Club had enough evidence to sweep Lucy's lies away once and for all.

The police were at the house through most of the day. Some plain-clothed officers took over Susan's study for a couple of hours while other officers cordoned off the chapel door with black and yellow tape so that no one could get in.

The three girls spent the day in the armoury, eager to see if Lucy would sneak in there and use the passage to the chapel.

Holly's hope was that the mysterious man was still hidden in there with the sword. After all, he couldn't have come out of the passage through the armoury exit. Holly's only fear was that there was another way out and that the man had already fled with the sword.

'I don't think he can have done,' said Belinda as the three of them sat morosely on the large black chest. 'There's a lot of empty land round the house. He'd have had to run a long way in the open to get clear.'

'That's right,' said Tracy. 'And that sword isn't the sort of thing you could put in your pocket. Belinda's right. The man *and* the sword are still here.'

The girls were briefly interviewed one by one by the police. Tracy and Belinda were able to say they hadn't seen a thing, and even Holly managed to answer truthfully that she didn't know anything. *After all*, she thought, *I don't know what happened, and there's no point in telling the police about what I suspect until there's some way of proving it!*

Tracy knelt on the chest with her elbows on the window-sill, gazing mournfully out over the lawns of Wylde House. The sun was high in a clear blue sky and birds were swooping and diving in the air. Over to the right she could see the chapel, its door locked and barred by police tape.

Their lengthy vigil in the armoury was beginning to get her down.

Holly and Belinda were sitting cross-legged on the floor, playing yet another game of The Mystery Chase with their home-made board and pieces.

'You win, again,' sighed Belinda as Holly's piece

landed on the centre square and the secret documents were delivered safely to the prime minister. She looked over her shoulder. 'Tracy? Do you fancy joining in again?'

'Not really,' sighed Tracy. She turned round. 'Lucy isn't going to try using the passage in broad daylight, is she?' she said. 'Can't we go out for a while? Look at that sun. It's lovely out.'

'I'm not leaving this room unguarded,' said Holly. 'You can go for a walk if you want to.'

Tracy slipped down on to the floor with her friends. 'I guess not,' she said. 'Come on, then; give me the dice. Let's throw for who starts.'

It was an hour or so later that Susan came into the armoury. She looked pale and stressed, but there was no sign in her face that she was still concerned about the awkward confrontation between Holly and Lucy.

'What are you three doing cooped up in here?' she asked. 'The police have gone, you know. You can go out if you want to.'

'We're fine in here, thanks,' said Holly.

Susan looked at their game. 'Did you make that yourselves?' she said. 'That's very clever of you. What's it all about?'

Susan crouched down as the three friends explained the board-game. 'And what's that?'

asked Susan, pointing to a particular square. On it was written: 'You use a "Miranda" disguise and are spotted immediately. Miss a turn.'

'Miranda is a friend of mine,' explained Holly. 'She used to like wearing these really silly disguises.'

There was more that Holly could have told Susan, but she thought better of it. Miranda Hunt and Peter Hamilton were friends from the days when Holly lived in London. They had called themselves the Mystery Kids and had plenty of extraordianry adventures long before Holly's family had moved up to Yorkshire and Holly had set up the Mystery Club.

But this didn't seem to Holly to be the appropriate time to tell Susan of her fascination with mysteries. That could wait until the secret passage was opened and the whole story could come out.

'Do the police have any idea of what happened?' Belinda asked Susan.

'They think someone must have bypassed the alarm,' sighed Susan. 'They've had a long talk with poor old Tom.' She shook her head. 'I think he feels worse about it than I do. It must have been done last night.' She stood up. 'But the police are hopeful that it'll turn up.'

Holly noticed that Susan seemed to have forgotten that she had mentioned seeing the sword just before Tom discovered the theft.

'Will you have to cancel the Children's Masquerade?' asked Tracy.

'No,' said Susan. 'This will put a bit of a damper on it, of course, but I phoned John to tell him what had happened and he says we should go on with the Masquerade.' She gave the three girls an unhappy look. 'Actually, I still haven't phoned the museum. Lord only knows what they're going to say about all of this.'

'Is there anything we can do to help?' asked Holly.

'I don't think so, thank you,' said Susan. 'Just try to keep out of Lucy's way. I understand why you aren't getting along with her, but she really isn't such a bad girl underneath.'

Susan left the room.

'I'm not looking forward to telling Susan about Lucy,' said Holly in an undertone.

'She's got to be told,' said Belinda.

'Yes, I know,' said Holly.

It was only a few minutes later that Susan came back into the room. She was carrying a small wooden box.

'Seeing that you seem to like games and puzzles,'

she said. 'I thought this might keep the three of you occupied for a while.'

She handed the box to Belinda. It was about thirty centimetres long by ten wide and ten deep, covered all over with carved patterns and designs in different coloured wooden inlays.

'It's lovely,' said Belinda, turning the exquisite box over in her hands. 'What's it for?' She searched for a catch to open it. 'And how do you get into it?'

'That's the whole point,' said Susan. 'It's called a Chinese box, and there's only one way to get it open.'

'How?' asked Tracy, leaning over Belinda's arm.

'I'm not telling you that,' said Susan. 'You work it out for yourselves.'

'Was it actually made in China?' asked Holly, leaning forwards to look at the designs that covered it.

'No, Tom made it,' said Susan. 'He's very clever at things like that. Well, I'll leave you to it. I've got to phone the museum now and let them know what's happened.'

The three girls spent a long time puzzling over the box without any luck. Whatever the secret was, Tom Catchpole had certainly hidden it brilliantly.

Dinner-time approached and they realised that

they would have to leave the armoury unguarded. Holly was concerned that the moment they turned their backs, Lucy would be in there to let her accomplice out. Then they would hide the sword somewhere where the Mystery Club would never be able to find it.

'Wait here,' said Belinda. 'I've got an idea.'

She ran out, returning from her room a few minutes later with a couple of strips of sticking plaster and a length of thread.

'My mum insisted that I should bring some plasters in case of accidents,' said Belinda. 'She's like that. And she got me to bring a needle and thread in case any buttons fell off.' She grinned. 'Useful, huh?'

'Useful for what?' asked Tracy.

'Well,' said Belinda, 'we can't stay in here all evening, but we can rig something up so we'll know if the passage has been used.' She looked at her two friends. 'That's better than nothing, isn't it?'

Belinda ducked into the fireplace and fixed the thread across the side wall, low near the ground so that the plasters wouldn't be noticed.

'There you are,' she said. 'If anyone comes in or out of the passage, the thread will be pulled away.'

'And I guess at least we'll know for certain that the entrance is in here,' said Tracy.

'I already know for certain,' said Belinda.

'But knowing isn't enough,' said Holly. 'We've got to be able to prove it.'

With their warning system in place, the three girls left the armoury and tidied themselves up for dinner with Susan.

There was no sign of Lucy. It was all very well setting up a device to show that the passage had been used, but it wouldn't really help them to track the missing sword down, or to prove that Lucy was involved in the theft.

Holly's anxiety was relieved when Tracy noticed that Lucy's car was missing from the drive. Obviously Lucy had gone out.

'Did you have any luck with the box?' asked Susan as they ate their meal.

'I don't think it opens at all,' said Tracy.

'It does, you know,' said Susan, putting her knife and fork down. 'Give it to me for a moment.'

Belinda handed the box over. Susan made several swift, deft moves with her hands and the lid of the box sprang open.

Holly gaped at her. 'How did you do that?'

'It's quite easy, really,' said Susan. They craned forwards while Susan showed them the exact series of twists and turns and pushes needed to loosen the lid of the box.

'You see?' she said. 'The trick is to do two different things at the same time, otherwise none of it will operate. I said that Tom's clever.' Her eyes stared into the distance. 'I only wish his son took after him.' She shook her head as though to dismiss her thoughts.

'I'm really sorry about the trouble with Lucy earlier,' said Holly.

'Let's not talk about that,' said Susan. 'I think we should just try and forget all about it. You just got off on the wrong foot, that's all. Don't let it spoil the rest of your stay.'

After dinner, the three girls helped Susan clear up in the kitchen. A quick check in the armoury showed that their tripwire had not been broken.

'If anything's going to happen,' said Belinda, 'It'll happen tonight, when everyone's supposed to have gone to bed.'

'Which means we don't go to bed, I guess,' said Tracy. 'What are we going to do? Take turns down here to keep watch?'

'I think so,' said Holly. 'We'll each watch for three hours. But we mustn't try to catch Lucy or the man. What we want to know is how to get into the passage, and anything we can overhear about what they've done with the sword.'

Lucy arrived back at the house some time in the late evening, slamming doors and running straight up to her room without even saying hello to her mother.

It wasn't long before the three friends said goodnight to Susan and headed up to their rooms. They had tossed coins to decide the order in which they would watch. Belinda first, until two in the morning, then Tracy until five, and finally Holly from five until eight the following morning.

Belinda crept back down to the darkened armoury. She felt carefully in the chimney and found that the thread was still undisturbed. Then she crept across the floor and slid down into the gap between the black chest and the wall.

She did her best to make herself comfortable, lying on her side with the top half of her head, from the eyes upwards, sticking out from behind the chest. It gave her a perfect view of the chimney breast. She rested her head on her arm and prepared herself for a long wait.

Belinda awoke with a start, banging her head on the edge of the chest as she jerked out of a sleep she had no memory of drifting into. Calling herself names under her breath, she looked at her watch. It was just past midnight and perfectly silent. She had lost almost an entire hour.

She could just imagine what Holly, and especially Tracy, would have to say about that! And the way Belinda usually slept, a whole herd of elephants could have marched out of the secret passage without waking her.

She was about to get up and creep over to the fireplace to check on the thread when she heard a stealthy sound. Her ears pricked and she held her breath. The sound came again. The soft, slow creak of shoes on the bare boards of the armoury floor.

She edged her head round the side of the chest. There, caught in the full moonlight, all in black save for the white-blonde cascade of her hair, was Lucy Fanshaw. And as Belinda watched in breathless silence, Lucy tiptoed across to the fireplace and ducked in under the low arch.

8 A perilous night out

Lucy crouched in the arch of the fireplace. This was the moment that Belinda had been waiting for. The moment when the secret of the entrance to the passageway would be revealed.

Lucy lifted one arm high and pressed her palm against the keystone of the arch. At the same time, she reached across and took hold of a brick near the floor. She gasped at the effort as she gave the lower brick a fierce twist while pressing hard upwards against the keystone. From within the fireplace came a gritty scraping sound.

Tap! *Tap*! The noise came suddenly and utterly unexpectedly from just above Belinda's head. The sharp sound of fingernails rattling on glass. Lucy's head jerked around and a look of recognition came over her face as she stared through the window directly above where Belinda was hiding.

Lucy leaned into the fireplace and seemed to be pushing. There was that scraping sound again.

Lucy was closing the entrance to the secret passage. And then, to Belinda's horror, Lucy came running over to the window.

Don't move, thought Belinda. *Don't move a muscle. You might still get away with it*.

'Meet me at the front door,' she heard Lucy say, speaking in that very slow and precise way that people do when they mean their words to be lip-read rather than heard.

Whoever was outside the house must have understood what she had said, because Lucy ran immediately across the room and out through the door.

Belinda wormed her way out from behind the chest. She felt stiff and sore from her hour on bare boards, but there was no time to massage her aching muscles. She had to find out what was going on.

But as she tried to stand up she realised that her left foot had gone to sleep. Her foot felt like a lump of lifeless rubber attached to the end of her leg. It flopped to one side as she put her weight on it and she fell sprawling on the floor.

She lay quite still, convinced that at any moment Lucy would appear back at the armoury door to see what had made the noise. But Lucy didn't reappear.

Belinda sat up, nursing her foot in both hands as the blood began to flow back into it and the sensation of lifelessness was replaced by the maddening burn of pins-and-needles.

Belinda stood up carefully. She had wasted precious time on her stupid foot, and she couldn't afford to stand around until the tingling was gone. She ran forwards in an off-balance lope.

She was afraid that Lucy might already have slipped off into the night with the mysterious tapper-at-the-window. But as she slowed and crept nearer the main hall of the house, she could hear voices. She pressed herself tight against the wall and strained to listen.

'What do you mean, it's already been stolen!' That was a male voice. A young man's voice.

'Be quiet!' Lucy's voice this time. 'Those three kids are suspicious about us. We can't talk here, I think one of them might be keeping watch. Go to the watch tower. I'll meet you there in an hour. We'll be able to talk without anyone overhearing us.'

'The watch tower?' The young man's voice sounded surprised. 'But—'

'Shhh!' Lucy's hiss silenced the man and then she said something in a low voice that Belinda was unable to make out.

'OK,' said the man. 'Got you. One hour. I'll be there.'

The front door was quietly closed and Belinda edged herself even deeper into shadows as she saw Lucy walk across the hall and patter quietly up the stairs.

Belinda gave Lucy a minute or two to get well out of the way before she went limping on her tingling foot over to the staircase and headed up to the bedrooms.

She got Holly out of bed first and the two of them went along to Tracy's room.

'I've seen how the passage opens,' said Belinda. 'But there's something strange going on. For a start, the man wasn't in the passage – he was outside the house. And he sounded really shocked about the sword having been stolen.'

'Maybe Lucy stole it without telling him,' said Holly.

'She can't have done,' said Tracy. 'At the same time as the sword was being stolen, Lucy was busy locking me in that attic. There's no way she could have got all the way down to the armoury and into the passage.'

'She couldn't have done it at all,' said Belinda. 'Don't forget, I was in the armoury. Unless, of course, there's another entrance somewhere else in the house. That's the only explanation. But listen, Lucy and the man have arranged to meet at the watch tower in an hour.'

'They did what?' Holly said in surprise. 'Why the watch tower, for heaven's sake?'

'Lucy was suspicious that one of us was lurking about listening,' said Belinda. 'She wanted to meet somewhere where we wouldn't be able to overhear them.' Belinda looked at her two friends. 'If we want to find out what's going on, we've got to go to that watch tower.'

'Wait a minute,' said Holly. 'What about the tide? Is it in or out now?'

'It must be out,' said Tracy. 'How else could Lucy and that man meet there?' Tracy's eyes sparkled in the light of her bedside lamp. 'Hey, that tower would be the perfect place to hide the sword. Maybe that's why they're going there.'

'But the man didn't know the sword was missing,' insisted Belinda.

'I've got it!' said Holly. 'It's simple. They were planning on stealing the sword together, right? But then Lucy must have realised we were on to her, so she jumped the gun. She lured Tracy out of the way, got into the secret passageway through a *different* entrance and took the sword without the man's help. I'll bet you ten million pounds that

Lucy's got the sword hidden somewhere in the house. She's arranged to meet the man at the watch tower for precisely the reason Tracy just mentioned. The watch tower would be a great place to hide the sword.' She looked at the two of them. 'Well? Does it make sense?'

'You bet it does!' said Tracy. She jumped fully clothed out of bed. 'Well?' she said. 'What are you waiting for? We need to get to that watch tower before they do!'

It was exciting to think that they were so close to solving the mystery of the theft. If Holly's theory was right, they'd have the whole thing sewn up before the first light of dawn. And they didn't even need to catch Lucy and the man red-handed. All they needed to do was hide themselves at the tower, see where the sword was put, and then retrieve it and take it back to Susan with the whole story.

The sky was ablaze with stars as the three girls left the house and made their way down the slope of the hillside towards the bridge that crossed the River Wrath. The night was so still and calm that they could clearly hear the soft swish of the distant waves on the beach.

They stood at the near side of the low stone

bridge. Beneath them the waters of the river swirled loudly, the noise echoing under the dark arch. A channel of large boulders marked the landward side of the river beyond the bridge, marching down along the beach. At high tide all that could be seen of these stones was their tips rising above the water, but now they were clear of the water, standing high on the edge of the low, flowing river in shadowy pools ringed with seaweed and green algae.

The sharp salt smell of the sea filled their nostrils as the three girls slid down off the road and made their way out on to the long, smooth stretch of sand that led to the watch tower.

'Remember what Susan said,' warned Belinda. 'Keep to the sandbanks where it's firm.'

But it wasn't quite as easy as that as they headed towards the tall, crook-backed hump of the ruined watch tower. The beach rose and fell in long undulations. In places their way forward was barred by long silvery threads of water and in other places they found themselves unable to avoid the soft, yielding sand that threatened to suck their shoes off.

But it didn't take them long to reach the watch tower. They crunched through tiny shells and shingle and climbed on to the grassy shoulders of the small island. The grass was long and wiry, perfect for giving hand-holds as they clambered up the steep rocks and found themselves in the shadow of the broken old tower.

At its highest, it rose no more than three metres above the rocks, its massive stone walls cracked and ruined and overgrown with moss and lichen. It was a simple structure; a circular wall about a metre thick with the remains of a stone spiral staircase within.

'Spooky!' whispered Tracy as she led them through a low, arched doorway into the rubble-strewn floor of the tower.

Holly looked round. The brittle-edged shape of the broken walls rose and fell around them, black against the sky.

Tracy climbed the stairs, her head lifting above the highest point of the walls.

'Keep down!' said Holly. 'You'll be seen.'

'Oh, yeah, sorry,' said Tracy, ducking down. She came back to where Belinda and Holly were standing. 'There's a whole bunch of lights on the horizon,' she said.

'I think they're fishing boats,' said Holly. 'I've seen them before. What's the time?'

'A quarter to one,' said Belinda. 'And it was just gone twelve when Lucy said they'd meet here in an hour. Which means they could be here any time now. We need to find somewhere to hide.'

'There aren't a whole lot of choices,' said Tracy, looking around. 'Unless we can lift a rock and hide under it.'

'Let's just get round to the seaward side outside the wall,' said Holly. 'At least we know they won't approach from that direction.'

They came out through the archway again and made their way carefully over the rubble and debris round to the far side of the tower. They managed to find reasonably comfortable places to sit and wait.

'I still can't figure out who Lucy's accomplice is,' said Holly as they gazed out over the shimmering ripple of the sea. 'If her boyfriend is in Manchester, who has she found to help her?'

'*If* he's in Manchester,' said Belinda.

'He must be,' said Holly. 'Tom said he spoke to him on the phone this morning. There's no way Colin could have got back here quickly enough to be involved.'

'But did Tom say who phoned whom?' asked Belinda.

'What difference does that make?' asked Tracy.

'A whole lot of difference if Colin phoned Tom,'

said Belinda. 'A person could phone from two streets away and say he was in Manchester.'

'Oh!' breathed Holly. 'I hadn't thought of that.'

'We can't all be brilliant,' said Belinda. She looked at her watch. It was ten minutes past one. 'They're late,' she said.

'We'd better keep really quiet from now on,' Holly said softly. 'We can't risk them hearing us talking and making a run for it.' She shivered, beginning to feel a chill despite the balmy warmth of the night.

The three girls huddled together against the cool breeze that had struck up off the sea.

'Shall I take a quick look over the top?' Tracy suggested some time later. 'To see if anyone's coming?'

'OK,' said Holly, stifling a yawn. 'But try to keep your head as low as possible.'

The long wait was making all three of them sleepy, and it was only the sharp breeze that kept them alert.

Tracy climbed the rocks and edged her head up over the wall.

'I don't want to worry anyone,' Belinda said quietly, 'but I've been watching the tide. It's coming in, you know.'

Holly looked out at the waves that gently lapped

the sand in front of them. The sea was certainly nearer to the tower, but still fifty or so metres away from the small island.

'And it's almost two o'clock now,' said Belinda. 'Do you know what I think? I think we've been conned again.'

'I don't see how,' said Holly. 'OK, so Lucy was suspicious that we might be keeping a watch on her, but why would she say to meet here unless she meant it?'

Belinda looked unhappily at Holly. 'I think she might have heard me,' she said. 'I'm beginning to think she knew I was there. She whispered something to the man after she mentioned about meeting here. I'll bet she said for him to play along with her because they were being overheard.' Belinda looked at Holly. 'I sort of forgot to mention that I fell over in the armoury. She must have heard me.'

'You fell over!' exclaimed Holly.

'It wasn't my fault,' said Belinda. 'My foot went to sleep.'

'Oh, marvelous!' said Holly. 'Now she tells us! Tracy! Forget looking out for Lucy. We've been wasting our time!'

'Uh, I think you guys should look at this,' came Tracy's voice from the wall. She had climbed right up on to the broad top and was staring landwards.

Holly and Belinda climbed up after her.

'Oh, my gosh!' gasped Holly, her hand coming up to her mouth.

A broad stretch of grey water covered the sand between the island and the mainland.

'How did that happen?' breathed Belinda.

'Never mind how,' said Tracy. 'It's happened. The question is, what the heck are we going to do about it?'

They had been thrown off their guard by a peculiarity of the long beach. On the seaward side of the watch tower island, the exposed seabed rose in a long spit of sand, around which the waters of the incoming tide had been slowly pouring.

They had thought that the tide was still a long way out, but already the sea had seeped in round them, filling the lower channels and rising silently up over the sandbanks. All that remained above the swirling water were a few rounded humps of sand.

The rising tide had cut them off.

9 Narrow escape

'How deep do you suppose it is?' asked Holly. The silvery-grey sheen of the rising waters gave no hint of what lay beneath.

'It can't be too bad yet,' said Tracy. She pointed. 'Look, that's the way we came, and there are still plenty of sandbanks above the surface.'

'Yeah,' Belinda said darkly. 'But for how long?'

'We've got two choices,' said Holly. 'Either we stay here all night, or we try to wade ashore. But if we're going to try wading we'd better do it now. Before it gets too deep.'

'Perhaps we'd better stay,' said Belinda.

'I'm not sitting up here all night,' said Tracy. 'Come on, you guys. We'll easily get back, so long as we don't stand around here talking about it for hours.'

Tracy scrambled down to the narrow strip of shingle that was still visible above the flooding seawater.

Holly looked enquiringly at Belinda. Belinda gave her a morose look and shrugged before sliding down in Tracy's wake.

Tracy was leaning against a rock, undoing her shoes.

'There's no sense in getting them wet if we can help it,' she said.

In a couple of minutes all three girls had their shoes and socks in their hands and were at the water's edge with their jeans rolled up to their knees.

'I really love a nice paddle at two o'clock in the morning,' Belinda said miserably. 'I've been dying to try it out all week.'

'And whose fault is it that we're here?' said Holly. 'Who fell for Lucy's little trick?'

Belinda gave a rueful smile. 'You've got me there,' she said. 'Oh, well, it makes a change for me to get us into trouble. It's usually you or Tracy.'

'It is not,' said Tracy. 'I'm the one who gets us out of trouble.'

'You better had this time,' said Belinda. 'I really don't fancy having to swim back.'

'OK,' said Tracy. 'Here goes. I'm pretty sure I remember the way. Just follow me.'

She stepped into a swirl of water.

'*Ooh*! Cold!' she said.

Holly and Belinda followed her, each surprised by the chill of the water as it flowed over their ankles.

At first the seabed seemed fairly level, the sand only occasionally dipping into a trough that brought the water halfway up the girls' shins.

'It's freezing!' moaned Belinda. 'I think my toes have dropped off!'

'It's getting shallower,' said Tracy. They came up out of the water on to a long bank of soft sand. 'Oh, help!' Quite unexpectedly Tracy found that the sand gave way beneath her feet, plunging them into holes almost to her knees.

But it wasn't like quicksand. It was quite firm, like freshly fallen snow, and as the three of them plodded awkwardly across the sandbank they left a trail of deep pits.

'This way,' said Tracy, leading them back into shallow water and rippled sand that was hard as iron under their feet.

'Ow! Ow! Ow!' exclaimed Belinda. 'This is murder on my poor feet. Are you sure this is the best way?'

'Stop moaning,' said Tracy. 'I'm doing my best.'

There was another sandbank ahead. One long, low bank, and then a smaller round dome of sand,

and then a gap before the last bank that would virtually take them to the shore.

Tracy waded towards the first sandbank. The rushing water rose up her legs, splashing round her knees and wetting the roll of her jeans. But more alarming than that was the uncomfortable way the water seemed to be tugging at her feet.

'There's quite an undercurrent here,' she said, looking round at her friends. 'Careful it doesn't trip you.'

But that was the deepest part and soon all three of them were on dry land again.

Tracy looked for the dome of sand towards which she had been aiming. It was gone. The tide had already risen to cover it. And she noticed that the final sandbank was smaller than it had been only a few minutes ago.

'Not far to go now,' Tracy said encouragingly. 'Another fifty metres and we'll be home!'

She waded into the water but was alarmed to feel the seabed falling sharply away beneath her feet. The water was swooshing round her knees again and still the seabed was dropping. And the currents were stronger than ever.

'This isn't going to be so easy,' she said. 'I think we'd better join hands. We're going to get wet, I'm afraid.'

Belinda took Tracy's hand and Holly linked on at the end. As she waded deeper and deeper, Holly was shocked by how strong the pull of the tide was. After only a few steps she was up to her knees and every lift of a leg brought with it the danger of being swept off her feet.

All around them was the hiss and swish of the tide, like whispering, warning voices. More ominously, from the dark line of the cliffs, came the angry rush of waves breaking on rocks. Holly did not find it a very reassuring sound.

The water was halfway up Tracy's thighs when she hit a patch of soft, sucking sand and felt the porridgey goo, all slimy through her toes.

'It's no good,' she said. 'We'll have to go back. It's getting deeper all the time, and it's really horrible down here.'

They turned back and Holly led them up on to the sandbank again. Even in that short space of time the shoreline had receded and their haven had shrunk by half its length.

'If anyone has any fantastic ideas,' said Tracy, 'now would be a really good time to share them with us.'

'Could we swim for it?' suggested Holly.

'Have you any idea how heavy waterlogged clothes get?' said Tracy. 'And the undertow is really fierce.'

'I'm getting just a tiny bit anxious about this,' said Belinda. 'Would someone come up with a brilliant plan, please?'

A particularly large wave came flooding over the sandbank where they were standing.

'This way,' said Holly, heading along the bank.

'But that's the opposite direction from where we want to go,' said Tracy.

'I know,' said Holly, 'but there are some other ridges over there. Maybe we can sort of zigzag our way back.'

'I'm with Holly,' said Belinda. 'We've got to do something.'

To begin with it looked as though they were making good progress. The sandbank was twenty or more metres long, and there was only a shallow dip under the water before they came to another bank which curved a little way nearer the shore. And Holly was right about one thing: in this direction there seemed to be more land above the rising waterline.

Where the sand was hard and firm, the three girls were able to run. But every time they seemed to be making any progress towards the line of boulders that marked the edge of the river, they were thwarted either by deep treacherous water or by the sort of slimy sand that crawled up unpleasantly around their ankles and seemed to have no firm bottom.

Steadily, they were being driven further from the river and nearer to the sheer drop of the cliffs.

'This is crazy!' shouted Tracy as Holly and Belinda plunged into yet another channel of rushing water. 'We're going to be trapped if we keep going this way!'

She looked round and her heart sank. Already most of the dark humps over which they had come were gone under the greedy foam of the tide. There was no safe way back.

She ran to catch up with Holly and Belinda, sending up plumes of water as she fought through a racing sea that reached almost to her waist. She grabbed Belinda's outstretched hand and the three of them struggled onwards as the deep, cold undertow tugged remorselessly at their freezing feet.

The cliffs loomed above them, ghostly white in the dark of the night. Holly gave a cry of relief as she felt the seabed rising. In only a dozen or so steps all three of them were out of the water and on a high fist of rock under the sheer side of the cliff towering twenty metres over their heads.

'At least . . . we're on . . . dry land. . . .' Holly panted, exhausted from her fight with the sea.

'For the time being,' gasped Belinda. She pointed

to a green line on the cliff face, just visible in the darkness. The line of high tide. It was almost at their chest height.

It seemed that their respite from the sea was only temporary. And even as the three friends tried to come to terms with this latest shock, a huge wave broke over the rock, spattering them with brine.

'What's that?' said Tracy, spitting out seawater and pointing a little way along the cliff. The phantom grey of the cliff was broken by a dark slit. And now that the girls looked more closely, they could see that there were several of these black gouges in the cliff face.

'Is it some sort of cave?' asked Belinda. Holly made her way over the slippery rock towards the crack. She leaned into the hole. It was four or five metres high, and easily wide enough to step into, although she couldn't see where it could possibly lead them.

She stepped carefully into the gash, feeling firm rock or earth beneath her feet. Another step forwards took her into complete darkness, but the sides of the gulf became no narrower, and the rocky floor seemed to rise quite steeply in front of her.

She backed out and called to the others. 'Remember those holes we almost fell into up on top of the cliff?' she said. 'I've got a feeling these might be where they lead to.'

'You mean we can climb up them?' said Tracy.

'I'm not certain,' said Holly. 'But it's got to be worth a try.' Another huge wave crashed on the rocks, soaking the three girls from head to foot.

Holly wiped her face with her wet sleeve. 'Do you two want to wait here while I try it out?'

'No way!' said Belinda. 'I'm not staying here waiting to be knocked off by the next big wave.'

Holly went back into the cleft, feeling with hands and feet in the blackness as she climbed.

Tracy was the last to enter the chasm, and even as she did so a wave came crashing in a huge spume of foam at her back. Another couple of waves like that and they really would have been swept away into the sea.

It was unnerving for Holly, climbing blindly up into the cliff with no certainty that the chasm wouldn't simply come to an end and force them to go back. It was like tunnelling up through a narrow tube, but there were plenty of hand-holds and footholds. Occasionally her foot would loosen a clump of something and she would hear a yell of annoyance from Belinda as she was hit.

At one point the sides of the chasm narrowed alarmingly and Holly was afraid that the worst had happened: the tunnel was going to taper to a point and be unpassable. But she was determined not to give in just yet. She twisted her shoulders and dug her feet in, pushing up through the invisible barrier. She gave a gasp. There was cold air on her face.

Down below, Belinda and Tracy heard a muffled shout from Holly.

'What's she saying?' panted Tracy.

'I don't know,' said Belinda. 'Hey! Holly! What's wrong?' Belinda reached up and caught hold of Holly's foot. A second later the foot was lifted up out of her reach and Holly let out another triumphant shout.

'I'm out!'

The narrowing of the passage was the final obstacle before Holly found her head lifting up through long stringy grass. The wonderful brilliance of the star-filled night sky wheeled above her.

It wasn't long before all three girls were safe on the cliff top, clinging on to one another in relief.

Only a few hundred metres away they could see the long dark shape of Wylde House. Their desperate ordeal was over.

They were too exhausted to feel elated by their escape. All three of them were saturated with seawater; cold and desperately tired. And it didn't help to think that it had been Lucy Fanshaw who had tricked them into that situation.

Not that they supposed Lucy had meant for them to be in any real danger. All the same, Holly felt a grim determination not to allow that sly young woman to fool them a third time. Twice was more than enough!

They made their way silently through the darkened house, creeping together into the bathroom and peeling off their wet clothes before stepping one by one under a hot shower.

Wrapped in towels they made the final effort of running quietly to their rooms.

'Don't sleep in,' Holly whispered to the others. 'We've got to investigate that passage tomorrow.'

Belinda groaned and shook her head. 'Haven't you had enough?' she moaned. 'I just want to sleep. And then, when I've finished sleeping, I want to turn over and sleep some more. And then, when I've—'

'I think we get the picture,' said Tracy with a tired grin. 'See you in the morning.'

Holly slid into bed and fell almost immediately into a deep, dreamless sleep.

* * *

Holly was awoken early the next morning by the clamour of voices below her bedroom window. Blearily, and only half awake, she staggered over to the window and yanked the curtains open. Susan and a group of other people were gathered on the lawn. In the distance more people were busy with planks and boards and rolls of canvas. Boxes and crates were being carried here and there and several cars and vans were parked on the boundaries of the broad square area of grass between the nearby flower beds and the distant trees.

'The Children's Masquerade!' Holly said to herself as she rubbed the sleep out of her eyes. 'Of course!'

The actual festivities would not begin until tomorrow, but there was a great deal of preparatory work to be done, and by the look of the hive of activity in the grounds of Wylde House that morning, most of it was well under way.

Holly blinked and stared. A familiar blonde-haired head was busy down there, helping to carry a large roll of brightly coloured canvas. It was Tracy.

There was a feeble knock and Belinda dragged herself in through the door looking like the 'before' photo in a health food advertisement.

'Have you seen this?' asked Holly, pointing down to the athletic Tracy.

'I know,' said Belinda. 'Don't even talk about it. I don't know where that girl gets her energy from.' She looked Holly up and down. 'How are you feeling?'

Holly swung her arms experimentally. 'Not too bad. What happened to our wet clothes?' The last Holly remembered was dumping their clothes in a heap in the bathroom.

'Tracy's put them in the washing-machine,' said Belinda.

'Good job I brought some spare jeans,' said Holly. 'I suppose you're going to have to wear something other than that horrible old green sweat-shirt of yours for once.'

'Don't count on it,' said Belinda with a grin. 'You're not the only person who brought spares.'

Belinda went off to get dressed and the two girls met in the corridor. Belinda had on a replacement green sweat-shirt, almost exactly the same as the one in the wash.

'How many of those things have you got?' asked Holly as the two girls went down to the kitchen.

'A drawerful at home,' said Belinda. 'I like them.'

Holly smiled. 'You don't say!'

The back door of the kitchen was open and as

they ate breakfast they could see and hear all the activity outside.

Tracy came bouncing over the threshold, looking as fresh as a daisy.

'You're up at last,' she said. 'I was just coming to drag you out of bed.'

'Don't be so loud!' said Belinda.

'I'm not speaking loudly,' said Tracy.

'I didn't say you were,' said Belinda. 'You're being loud! You're being fit and healthy and totally sickening. Don't you ever get worn out?'

'Of course I do,' said Tracy. 'I just don't complain about it the way you do.' She looked out through the open door. 'I've been helping with the festival stuff,' she said. 'It looks like it's going to be great. Why don't you come and join in?'

'What about the armoury?' Holly said in a low, cautious voice. 'Is Lucy about?'

Tracy shook her head. 'Her car's gone,' she said. 'She's probably gone off somewhere to avoid helping out. Or to avoid coming face to face with us after the trouble she got us into last night.'

'Then this is probably a good time to go and take a look at that passage,' said Holly. 'While Lucy is in hiding and Susan is busy outside.'

They went along to the armoury.

'Can you remember how to open it?' Holly asked

134

as Belinda stood contemplating the fireplace, her chin in her hand.

'I'm just picturing what Lucy did,' said Belinda. She crouched under the arch. 'Now, if I remember correctly, she grabbed this.' Belinda lifted an arm and took a firm hold of the protruding base of the keystone. 'And then she did this.' Belinda stretched out and gripped a brick in the arch down near the floor. She gave the brick a wrench but nothing happened.

'Well?' said Tracy.

Belinda shoved upwards at the keystone but it didn't move.

'It's all a case of doing two things at once,' puffed Belinda from her strained position under the arch. 'Like Tom Catchpole's Chinese box.' She pushed and twisted simultaneously. She felt the keystone give a little and the side brick turned suddenly. There was a dry grating sound.

'Done it!' yelled Belinda.

Tracy and Holly ducked their heads in under the arch of the fireplace. The entire section of brickwork at the side of the fireplace had pivoted outwards to reveal the dark slot of a passage.

'It's really there,' breathed Holly, stepping forwards and edging herself past the brick doorway. She peered into the unfathomable darkness. 'We'll need a torch.'

'I've got a light on my keyring,' said Tracy. She took her keys out and pressed a switch on the tiny pencil-light. A little beam of clear white light shot into the tunnel.

'It's kind of narrow,' said Tracy, peering over Holly's shoulder.

'Can I have the torch?' asked Holly. Tracy handed it over and Holly let the pool of light roam and stretch over the dusty, cobwebby walls. The floor was of smooth stone, no more than fifty centimetres in width, and the tunnel seemed to thrust in a straight line to a flat wall of stone some five metres away.

Holly edged into the tunnel, Tracy just behind her.

'Belinda?' said Holly, 'do you want to stay here and keep watch?'

'No, I don't,' said Belinda. 'I want to see where this passage goes.'

So it was that the three of them sidled along the narrow passage, long cobwebs dangling in their faces and brushing against their hair. They followed the light that Holly held while the daylight through the entrance grew more and more weak.

Holly almost tripped on a jutting piece of metal in the floor. 'Careful here,' she warned the others as she stepped over it. She came to the wall that had seemed like the end of the passage and saw that the way ahead involved climbing down some very steep and uneven stone steps.

'We must be outside the walls of the house now,' said Holly as the three of them descended into a deeper section of the passageway. All around them was the musty smell of stale earth.

'I really think someone should go and keep an eye on the entrance,' said Holly.

'Meaning me, I suppose,' said Belinda. 'OK. I'll go back and take a quick look. But only if you two stay right here. I don't want you discovering things without me.'

'OK,' said Holly. 'We won't move.'

Belinda edged to the steep stone steps and climbed up, expecting at any moment to see the faint grey daylight of the open entrance. She climbed up into pitch darkness.

'Uh-oh!' she said softly as she edged along the black tunnel. She almost tripped on the metal protuberance in the floor. By now she should definitely be seeing the light from the armoury.

And then her hands struck a dead end.

The entrance was shut. She felt around for a release mechanism, but there was nothing on the rough brickwork or on the side walls. She pushed but the wall didn't give so much as a millimetre.

It was shut fast. There was no way back.

10 The priest's hole

Belinda carefully made her way down the steps of the cramped passageway and back into the small circle of light where her two friends were waiting.

'Do you want the good news or the bad news?' said Belinda.

'The bad news first,' said Holly.

'The wall has closed itself behind us and I couldn't find any way of getting it open,' Belinda said flatly.

'Marvelous!' breathed Tracy. 'And the good news?'

'I got back down the steps in the dark without breaking my neck,' said Belinda.

'It's not so bad,' said Holly. 'Maybe we'll be able to get out at the other end. And don't forget, if our theory about the theft of the sword is right, there must be other ways out.'

'So let's get on with it, shall we?' said Belinda. 'The air's not getting any fresher in here.'

138

Belinda was right about that. The air was musty and stale, like the air in a long disused cellar.

Holly nodded and began to sidle along the passage, illuminating their way ahead with the little keyring light.

'I hope the ceiling doesn't fall in,' said Tracy, staring up at the uneven stonework that formed a roof only a few centimetres above their heads.

'Did you have to say that just at this minute?' said Belinda.

'I can't help thinking things,' said Tracy.

'Maybe not,' said Belinda. 'But you can keep thoughts like that to yourself until we're out of here, can't you?'

'I won't say another word,' said Tracy.

They walked on for a few more seconds in silence.

'Do these walls look safe to you?' asked Tracy.

'*Tracy!*' Belinda and Holly yelled together.

'Sorr-ee!' said Tracy. 'How far do you think we've come?'

'Do you think we're under the chapel yet?' asked Belinda.

'Soon, I should think,' said Holly. The small light lit up another set of tall stone steps which pushed up into a well in the roof.

'This must be it,' said Holly.

She climbed the steps, rising up into a sort of chimney of old stone. There were seven steps. At the head of the last one was a wooden panel, about a metre square.

'What's going on?' Belinda called from the bottom of the stairs. 'Have you found anything?'

'Yes,' said Holly, guiding the torchlight all round the panel.

'There's got to be some way of getting this open,' she muttered. She gave the panel a push. 'Aha!' A rusted metal ring was set into the stonework at the bottom of the panel, and a bolt attached to the panel itself was engaged with the ring. Holly tugged at the bolt and it lifted easily. She pushed the door but it still refused to move.

'What's the hold-up?' asked Tracy. 'Do you want me to help?'

'No,' said Holly. 'I can manage. I've released the bolt, but there must be something else keeping it locked.'

'Maybe it opens towards you,' suggested Belinda. 'Have you tried that?'

Holly hauled at the bolt. 'Nope,' she said. 'That's not it.'

'Maybe it slides sideways?' said Tracy.

'Got any more ideas?' said Holly after trying both ways. 'Oh, hold on though.' She tugged upwards on the bolt and felt a movement. 'Ha! Got it!' The panel shifted upwards. Holly crammed her fingers underneath and pushed it right up. There was a click and the panel locked in place.

Holly had expected some light, but the hole left by opening the panel was quite dark. She thought it must either be an extension of the tunnel, or else somewhere without windows. Her heart jumped. The priest's hole!

She shone the light through and realised that the darkness was caused by some sort of thick material, like curtains, hanging over the hole. She pushed and the curtain moved. There was a burst of light from one side. Holly crawled through the hole and knelt up, drawing the material to one side.

Her eyes were dazzled by the light. She wasn't in the priest's hole, after all. She was in the chapel, blinking out from behind the old tapestry that covered the wall to the rear of the altar. Bright sunlight shone through the stained glass windows, dappling the interior of the chapel with a kaleidoscope of light. The wooden cross stood on its metal pedestal directly behind the altar. At the far end of the chapel Sir Brandon and Lady Eleanor lay, one pair of hands joined in endless prayer, the other cupped to hold the hilt of a sword that was no longer there.

'It's the chapel,' said Holly, coming out from behind the thick wall hanging to allow her two friends up out of the passageway.

'So you were right all along,' said Tracy. 'Wait until we tell Susan. That daughter of hers is going to get what's coming to her now, OK!'

Holly looked round at her. 'Think so?' she said.

'Sure,' said Tracy. 'What's the problem?'

'There wasn't another way out of the passage.' said Belinda.

'So?' said Tracy.

'So how did whoever stole the sword get it out?' said Holly. 'I saw it in here, right?' Ten minutes later Tom came in and found it missing. All that time, Belinda was in the armoury, and the three of us kept an eye on the armoury right through until dinner that evening. And when we went to dinner, we put that trip-wire up. No one went into or came out of the armoury entrance all that time.'

'They must have got out through the door here,' said Tracy.

'Not possible,' said Belinda. 'The police sealed it up. If someone broke the tape there would be some sign of it.'

'Then . . . then the guy must have been in the passage all the time,' said Tracy. 'Right up until when Lucy sent us on that wild-goose chase to the watch tower.' Tracy grinned. 'He must have got out then!'

'Tracy?' said Belinda.

'Huh?'

'Then who was it that Lucy was talking to when she mentioned meeting at the watch tower?' asked Belinda.

'Ah! Um, oh, rats!' said Tracy. 'OK, I give up. How did they do it, Holly? I bet you've worked it all out and you're just dying to tell us.'

'I don't have the slightest idea,' said Holly. 'I think we should get out of here and have a Mystery Club meeting right away.'

'You mean walk out through the sealed door?' said Belinda. 'Are you sure that's a good idea? Wouldn't it be better to keep all of this to ourselves until we've figured out the whole story?'

'How else do we get out?' asked Holly. 'You said the entrance in the armoury had closed itself.'

'Yeah, but there must be some way of getting it open from inside,' said Belinda. 'We should at least give it a try.'

'OK,' said Holly. 'We go back, then.'

'I'll lead this time,' said Belinda. 'Give me the light.'

Belinda eased herself back through the entrance

and down the tall steps. Holly came last, pausing to arrange the tapestry and let the panel down again.

They edged along the musty lower part of the passage and then up the steps.

'I quite like being in the lead for a change,' said Belinda, looking at Tracy over her shoulder.

'Watch where you're going,' said Tracy. 'Don't forget there's that – '

'*Yawhoop!*' wailed Belinda. The light went cartwheeling round the tunnel as Belinda tripped and fell flat on her face.

'– bit of metal sticking up,' Tracy finished. She put her hand over her mouth to stifle a giggle as Belinda glared up at her. 'Oh!' Tracy's laughter stopped as the torchlight shone on a black crack in the wall. An entire section of the stonework had moved inwards just a centimetre or so, but enough to show a dark slit.

'What's going on?' asked Holly.

'There's another way out,' said Tracy. 'Belinda tripped over that metal thing in the floor and a whole chunk of the wall moved.' Tracy pushed at the slant of the wall. Dust and dirt rained down on her but the stonework refused to move.

Belinda sat up. She added her strength to Tracy's and gradually they managed to force the entrance open.

'You were right again,' Tracy said to Holly. 'This must be how they got out!'

'Never,' said Belinda, getting to her feet and shining the light through the hole. Dust was still filtering down and their hands were covered in grime. 'This hasn't been used recently, you can see that. No one's disturbed this door for years and years.'

The torchlight showed a terribly cramped stone spiral staircase twining itself up through a vertical tunnel that didn't seem large enough to take a reasonably sized human being.

'Do we go up *there*?' Belinda asked dubiously.

'Of course!' said Holly. 'And you can lead.'

'I thought you might say that,' said Belinda. 'OK. Here goes.' She made her way up the staircase, spluttering and spitting as dust and grit fell down on her. The steps ahead of her were filmed with undisturbed dust. The stairway couldn't have been used for a *very* long time.

The winding stair seemed to go on and on, as though tunnelling its way right up through the house, and then, quite suddenly, Belinda found her way above blocked by a wooden trapdoor. She shoved at it and it opened in a torrent of dust and gravel and debris.

Coughing, Belinda heaved the trap until it fell backwards with a loud thump. She cast the light around.

'Well, well,' she said. 'Fancy that!'

It was a tiny room with only three walls, two of which were triangular due to a slope of wooden slats. It was only possible to stand up at one end of the room. The floor was of rough boards and along the tallest wall lay a wooden construction that the girls assumed was the base of a very narrow and uncomfortable-looking bed.

'The priest's hole!' said Holly as she climbed up after Belinda and Tracy and crouched on the floor with them.

'But no treasure,' said Tracy. 'Pity.'

Belinda shone the torch up at the sloping roof-wall. There seemed to be some kind of roughly made hatchway built into the planks.

'I wonder if that's a way out?' asked Belinda.

Holly turned in her crouched position. The hatch was held closed by two wooden catches which pivoted on rusty nails. She pulled the catches aside and pushed at the panel.

For the second time that morning, Holly was dazzled by sunlight as the hatch swung open on rust-brittle hinges along its upper side. In the full gleam of the sun, the tiny room seemed even more bleak and uninviting.

'Can you imagine what it must have been like?' said Tracy. 'Having to hide yourself away in here because people were trying to kill you?' She shook her head. 'It couldn't have been much fun being a priest in those days.'

'Can you see where we are?' asked Belinda.

Holly crawled out on to a narrow flat area bordered by a low red brick wall constructed like castle battlements. She lifted her head above the low wall and let out a gasp.

Below her the wide grounds of Wylde House spread, filled with activity as the preparations for the festival went on.

'We're on the roof,' Holly exclaimed. 'We've come out right up on the rooftop!'

Tracy followed her out. 'This is the second time I've been up here,' she said. 'And I know just how to get back into the house.'

Holly held the hatch open for Belinda to crawl out.

'It's a brilliant view,' said Holly.

'I don't want to know,' said Belinda. 'Just get me down from here.'

'Will do,' said Tracy. She looked round at the sloped roofscape. 'This way,' she said.

* * *

The three friends were sitting on Holly's bed. Holly had the Mystery Club's red notebook open.

'OK,' she said. 'We've proved the link between the armoury and the chapel, and we've proved that Lucy and the man she's working with know about it. Which means they both had access to the chapel. Unfortunately, we've also proved that Lucy and the man Belinda heard her talking to last night can't have used the passage to take the sword, because we know Lucy was busy leading Tracy astray at the time the sword was stolen, and that the man was outside the passage later that day and couldn't have had the chance to get out of the passage without us knowing.' Holly looked up. 'Is that right?'

'Whew! I'm impressed,' said Tracy. 'That was quite a mouthful!'

'It sounds about right to me,' said Belinda, lying on her back and nibbling at a bar of chocolate from the supply she'd brought with her from Willow Dale. 'So, where does that leave us? The sword goes missing at a time when Lucy couldn't have stolen it, and the man – whoever he is – couldn't have done it either. The sword couldn't have been stolen via the passage, or we'd have known about it. So, as Sherlock Holmes would say, dismiss the impossible and everything you have left, no matter how unlikely, must include the truth.'

'Did he really say that?' asked Tracy.

'I'm sure he said something along those lines,' said Belinda.

'Fair enough,' said Holly. 'But where does that leave us?'

'You definitely, positively, absolutely saw the sword in there that morning?' Belinda asked Holly.

Holly nodded. 'Definitely, positively, absolutely,' she said.

Belinda munched thoughtfully at her chocolate bar. 'Which means we have three possibilities, OK? One: the sword was taken out through the passage. Two: the sword was taken out through the main door of the chapel. Three: the sword wasn't taken out of the chapel at all.' She looked at her two friends. 'We know the passage can't have been used. So either the sword went out through the door or it didn't go out at all.'

'I'd have seen if anyone had been running away from the chapel with a sword that long in their hands,' said Holly.

'What about Tom?' asked Belinda.

'I think I'd have spotted it if he'd hidden it down his trouser-leg,' said Holly. 'He went in there empty-handed and he came out shouting a couple of minutes later, still empty-handed.'

'A couple of minutes later?' said Belinda.

'Well, a minute, say,' said Holly. 'Not long, that's for sure.'

'And you're certain he didn't have the sword hidden on him?' said Belinda.

'Don't be daft,' said Holly. 'What did you think he did with it? Folded it up and hid it in his shoe?'

Belinda sat up with a broad grin on her face. 'There you are then. Mystery solved by a simple process of elimination.'

'Sorry,' said Tracy, 'what did you say?' She looked at Belinda. 'You've solved the mystery? Did I fall asleep for a moment there and miss something important?'

'The sword is still in the chapel,' said Belinda. 'Picture the following scene. Tom arrives at the chapel. He goes in and does that thing with the alarm. Then he nips over to Sir Brandon's tomb, swipes the sword, hides it somewhere and comes running out, yelling that it's been stolen. The police assume the sword was stolen during the night and it never occurs to them to search the chapel. When the fuss dies down, Tom strolls back to the chapel, takes the sword from where he hid it and rides off into the sunset with it.' Belinda looked at the others.

'The perfect crime. Or it would have been, if not for the fact that Holly saw the sword just before Tom went into the chapel.'

'Wait a minute,' said Holly. 'I got the impression that Susan has known Tom for a long time. She trusts him. She got him to install the security system and everything. And you think he's the one who stole the sword?'

'I certainly do,' said Belinda.

'And what about Lucy and her friend?' said Holly. 'Do you think he was working with them?'

'I doubt it very much,' said Belinda. 'It's a sort of coincidence. Don't you see? I told you Lucy's mysterious friend was surprised when she told him the sword had already been stolen. Don't you get it? Tom nicked it before they had the chance! Lucy and whoever-he-is had nothing to do with it.' Belinda's eyes gleamed. 'Once you realise that, everything else falls into place. Tom Catchpole is the thief!'

11 A thief unmasked!

All three girls were talking at once; Belinda trying to convince them that her theory about Tom Catchpole was right, Tracy determined that Lucy must have had something to do with it, and Holly trying to make sense of all the notes she'd made, most of which now seemed redundant.

'Quiet!' Holly howled above the noise her two friends were making. 'I can't hear myself think!'

The argument subsided.

'I still say it was Tom!' murmured Belinda after a moment.

'Lucy!' said Tracy.

'Tom!' Belinda said, glaring as if to break the glass in her spectacles.

'Lucy!' said Tracy.

'You always have to have the last word!' exclaimed Belinda.

'No, I don't!' said Tracy. 'Besides, the only people

who ever say that are people who want to have the last word themselves, so there!'

'When the pair of you have quite finished,' Holly said, laughing as her friends squared up to each other, 'can we think properly about Belinda's idea?'

'I still say Lucy must have been involved,' said Tracy. 'Maybe the mysterious stranger was Tom!'

Holly shook her head. 'No, it was a younger man,' she said. 'I didn't get a really good look at him that night outside the chapel, but I'm sure it wasn't Tom.'

'And it wasn't Tom's voice I heard last night either,' said Belinda. 'It was a younger voice. A teenager.'

'Shall we leave that for the time being?' said Holly. 'Let's concentrate on Belinda's idea. If she's right, and Tom hid the sword in the chapel, then surely it must still be there? The police sealed the chapel off, so he can't have got back in there.'

'Unless he used the passage,' said Tracy.

'I'll bet anything you like that he doesn't even know the passage exists,' said Belinda. 'Think about it. If he knew there was a secret passage, why would he hide the sword in broad daylight? He could sneak in and spirit it away at dead of night. It'd be a lot less risky.'

'Which means the sword must still be somewhere in the chapel,' said Holly. 'There hasn't been the chance for him to remove it yet.'

'So at least you believe me,' said Belinda.

'Let's say it's the only theory that makes any sense at the moment,' said Holly. 'But we'd better try and prove it before we go to Susan with accusations about Tom. Susan already thinks we're a bit over-imaginative after that business with Lucy. Lord only knows what she'd think of us if we marched up to her and accused Tom of stealing the sword.'

'Let's go and search the chapel,' said Belinda. 'Right now!'

'Except that this time,' said Tracy, 'we'll jam something in the entrance to the passageway so it doesn't close on us. I don't especially fancy getting out via the roof again.'

'That should do the trick,' said Holly.

The three friends were in the passage at the side of the fireplace in the armoury. Holly was bringing up the rear, and she had just wedged a hairbrush between the doorway and the brick wall.

There was still a great deal of activity to be seen through the armoury windows, but fortunately everyone out in the grounds of Wylde House was too far away to notice the three girls as they ran across the floor and dived into the fireplace.

Tracy was leading this time, shining her pencil-light along the passage. They all remembered to step over the lever as they passed the open entrance to the spiral staircase and the priest's hole.

They went down the steps, and along to the second set of stairs and the wooden panel that gave access to the chapel.

'Keep away from the windows,' Holly warned as they came out into the open from behind the heavy old tapestry. 'We don't want to be spotted.'

Tracy looked round the chapel. 'OK,' she said to Belinda. 'Where's the Lady of Wrath, then?'

'Right,' said Belinda, making her way down the aisle and standing by the white stone tomb. 'Tom walks in and grabs the sword.' She did a pantomime of Tom Catchpole lifting the sword from Sir Brandon's chest. 'Now, he's only got a few seconds, so he can't put it anywhere elaborate.' She walked round the tomb. 'Maybe the top slides off?'

'Yuck!' exclaimed Tracy. 'For heaven's sake, Belinda – there are skeletons in there! It's creepy enough knowing they're lying there, without trying to take the lid off!'

Belinda gave the stone lid an experimental shove.

'It must weigh tons,' said Holly. 'I don't think he could have moved it.'

'Maybe not,' said Belinda. She began to examine carefully the stone floor all round the tomb, hoping to see some telltale gap or crevice which would reveal a likely hiding-place.

At the same time Holly searched in, under and around all the pews, even going so far as to peer up under the seats in case the sword had somehow been fixed there out of sight.

And while her two friends searched, Tracy had a thorough look all round the altar and behind the hanging. There were other wooden panels in the wall, but no amount of tapping, pushing or fiddling revealed another secret entrance or hidey-hole.

Belinda did her best to keep clear of the windows as she shifted her search to the walls of the chapel. But nowhere in the discoloured white paint that covered the plaster was there the least hint of a crack to show the existence of a cleverly secreted hiding-place.

After a while Belinda went and sat morosely on the front pew, her cheeks in her fists.

'I was sure it would be here,' she said as Holly sat next to her. She spread her arms wide. 'I mean, it's this long, for heaven's sake. How could anyone manage to sneak something so big out of here without being noticed?'

Tracy stood in front of them. 'I don't want to say I told you so,' she said, not unkindly, 'but this does kind of mess up your theory about Tom having stolen it.'

'Not true,' Belinda said determinedly. 'We just haven't looked in the right place yet. Let's think about this. The sword is about one hundred and twenty centimetres long, right? By about thirty centimetres across the hilt. So we need to think in terms of a hiding place that could take something that shape.'

Tracy folded her arms, tilting her head as she tried to think. 'So we're looking for something that's a kind of cross-shape, huh?' she said. 'Uh, Holly, why are you looking at me like that?'

Holly wasn't staring at Tracy. She was staring at something that lifted itself high above Tracy's shoulder.

Belinda followed the line of Holly's eyes. She was staring as though spellbound at the wooden cross behind the altar. The cross that Tom had made. The cross that lifted itself on its metal stand about two metres in height and a metre along the cross beam. The cross made from expertly jointed slats of wood to form a box-shape. A *hollow* box shape.

'Oh, wow!' breathed Belinda. 'It's been staring us in the face all the time.'

Tracy turned and realised what her two friends were talking about.

'Tom made that Chinese box that Susan showed us, didn't he?' said Holly, standing up and slowly circling the altar. She stood behind the cross, looking again at the masterfully jointed sections of wood. 'And he told us he'd donated this cross to the chapel.'

'It's big enough to fit the sword in,' said Tracy. 'But can we figure out how to get into it? Do either of you remember how Susan got that box open?'

'Not really,' said Holly. She ran her hands over the smooth wood. She felt all round the cross as high as she could reach, hoping for some unevenness or movement that would give her some clue as to how it might open.

'Found anything?' asked Tracy after a minute or two.

'Give me a chance!' Holly realised she had sounded more irritated than she had intended. She gave Tracy a rueful smile. 'Sorry,' she said. 'This kind of thing drives me nuts.'

'Let me have a go,' said Belinda.

For the next ten minutes or so the three girls did their utmost to discover some way of opening the cross, but if it really did open, it was held shut by a mechanism that defied their best efforts.

'Maybe if we gave it a good whack with a hammer?' Belinda suggested, only half-joking.

'Oh, right,' said Tracy. 'And what if we find there's nothing in there? I'd like to hear you explain to Susan what you were doing. Correction, I'd like to be on a train home before you try explaining to Susan what you were doing.'

A sharp sound silenced them. A sound from the door near the other end of the chapel. Someone was trying to get in.

They gave each other a panicky look.

'It must be the police!' hissed Holly. 'Let's get out of here.' This was certainly no time to try and explain their presence in the chapel, or their half-formed theories about the theft of the sword.

They made a wild scramble for the entrance to the passage, Holly getting through last and rearranging the hanging to cover the hole. Belinda was at the bottom of the stairs in darkness, Tracy halfway up, and Holly at the top, listening intently.

There were no voices. She heard the scrape of the chapel door opening and then a second scrape as it was closed. In the general quiet she heard slow footsteps walk across the stone floor. A single set of footsteps that drew close and then stopped.

There was a grunt of breath and a thud, as if whoever had entered the chapel had dropped something heavy.

Holly couldn't stand it any more. She edged out of the square hole and very, very slowly brought her head to the side of the tapestry.

Tom Catchpole was standing with his back to her, looking up at the cross. On the floor by his foot was a long roll of green canvas.

As Holly watched, Tom reached out for the cross with both hands. His body was between her and the cross. It was impossible for her to see what he did, but a second later the whole of the back of the cross lifted away on a brilliantly hidden hinge at the very top.

Holly heard Tom gasp. It was a sound of pure shock as he looked into the hollow interior of the cross. Holly looked as well. Hanging by its hilt from the crossbeam was a sword. A long sword, about one hundred and fifty centimetres in length. But it wasn't the gleaming silver sword that went by the name of the Lady of Wrath.

It was a black sword with a time-eaten black blade and a simple black iron hilt lacking any sort of ornamentation. There was no glint of shining metal, nor any sparkle of jewels in the hilt. Whatever sword it was that lay hidden in

Tom Catchpole's Chinese box of a cross, it wasn't the Lady of Wrath.

And it was clear to Holly that Tom Catchpole was ten times more shocked at seeing the black sword than she was.

He seemed paralysed with amazement, holding the back of the cross up in one hand and almost panting as he stared at the sword. Then he let the false back come down. His hands made the same unseen motions as before and he stepped away from the now closed and inscrutable cross.

Holly had no idea what he might do next. It was obvious that he had expected to find the Lady of Wrath, and that someone had switched the priceless heirloom for a sword no different to several that adorned the armoury wall.

Tom lowered himself to the ground and sat cross-legged on the stones, his chin in his hands as he stared up at the cross.

Holly felt fingers plucking at her jeans. She batted the questing hand away, hoping that Tracy would have the sense to keep silent and still.

It seemed like an age before Tom finally stood up. He bent and lifted the roll of canvas and walked slowly towards the chapel door. As he opened the door he took a last look back down the length of the chapel to the altar. Holly was afraid that he would spot the top half of her head poking out from behind the tapestry, but Tom only had eyes for the cross. There was a grim look on his face, coupled with something that Holly took to be deep anxiety.

He closed the door behind him and Holly was at last able to take a proper breath.

'Has he gone?' whispered Tracy.

'Phew! Yes,' said Holly.

'Did he take the sword?' Belinda's voice came up from the bottom of the stairs. 'Shouldn't we get after him? Call the police? Tell Susan? Do something?'

'You're not going to believe what I just saw,' said Holly. 'We'd better go somewhere where we won't be disturbed.'

'Wasn't the sword in there, then?' asked Tracy as she backed down the steps to allow Holly through.

'Just give me a minute or two and I'll tell you all about it,' said Holly. 'Back in my room, where there's no fear of us being overheard.'

'The wrong sword?' said Tracy. 'What do you mean, the wrong sword? There is only one sword, Holly.'

The three girls were back in Holly's bedroom, Belinda and Tracy still completely baffled by Holly's revelations.

'Believe me,' said Holly, 'Tom was as shattered as you two. He must have gone in there to take the Lady of Wrath. He had a roll of canvas with him. He must have planned on taking the sword out of the cross, wrapping it up in the canvas, and just strolling out with it.'

'But isn't the chapel still sealed off?' asked Belinda. 'How did he get in?'

'I don't know,' said Holly. 'But the real question is, who switched the swords?'

'Someone who could get into the chapel without breaking the police seal,' said Belinda.

'Lucy!' Tracy almost squealed in her excitement. 'Lucy must have done it. Didn't I tell you? Didn't I say all along that Lucy would be involved? And you didn't believe me! You were both thinking, oh, it's only dumb old Tracy, don't take any notice of her. And I solved it! Lucy Fanshaw! Ha!'

'She had the chance to do it last night,' agreed Holly, somewhat more calmly than Tracy.

'If it was Lucy then she's got a heck of a lot of inside information,' Belinda said thoughtfully.

'What do you mean?' asked Holly.

'Well,' began Belinda, 'first, she knows how to work the entrance to a secret passage that's been lost for generations. Second, she knows how to disable Tom Catchpole's alarm system in the chapel. And now it looks as though she's able to figure out how to open that cross of Tom's. Either Lucy Fanshaw is some kind of total genius, or she's got to be the luckiest person in the world!'

'There's another possibility,' said Holly. 'She's getting some inside information. OK, so she could have stumbled over the passageway by accident, but she must have been told about the security system by someone.'

'Absolutely correct,' said Belinda. 'And if you ask me, it was the same person who told her how Tom Catchpole's cross opens.' She looked at the two of them. 'And would you like to take a few guesses as to who that might be?'

'You mean Tom?' said Tracy. She shook her head. 'That doesn't make any sense at all, Belinda.'

'No! Not *Tom*!' said Belinda. 'Colin! He'd be able to find out the code for the security system, I'm sure. And he's bound to know how his own father puts his trick boxes together.'

'So you think Lucy's accomplice is Colin after all?' said Holly. 'You don't think he went to Manchester?'

'I'm sure he didn't,' said Belinda. 'I'll bet you anything you like that it was Colin who phoned his father, and not the other way around. And I'll bet you anything else you like that Colin has been lurking round here ever since.'

'Let me get this straight,' said Tracy. 'Colin and Lucy were planning on stealing the Lady of Wrath, right? But Tom stole it first. And now Colin and Lucy have stolen it from Tom? Is that it?'

'In a nutshell,' said Belinda. 'Tom must have guessed how his father did it. He probably knew the cross was hollow and put two and two together. And then Lucy and Colin sneaked into the chapel last night and swapped the Lady of Wrath for an ordinary old sword.'

'So where's the Lady of Wrath now?' asked Tracy. 'And why did Lucy and Colin bother putting a different sword in the cross?'

'I don't know,' said Belinda. 'For some kind of weird joke, maybe.'

'You were up before either of us,' Holly said to Tracy. 'Was Lucy's car here earlier?'

'I don't remember seeing it,' said Tracy. 'Oh! I see what you mean. If they've got the sword, maybe they've run off with it.' Tracy frowned. 'No, I'm pretty sure the car was missing first thing this morning.'

'Then the pair of them have gone,' said Belinda. 'And they've taken the sword with them.' She scrambled off the bed. 'I think it's time we told

Susan the whole story. She's going to be devastated, but at least once she knows everything she'll be able to get the police on to it.'

'Agreed,' said Holly. 'And with any luck Lucy and Colin will be picked up before they get too far.'

The three girls headed out into the grounds of Wylde House in search of Susan Fanshaw. Despite the certainty in their minds that they had solved the mystery, they had no feeling of elation. It wasn't going to be much fun, telling Susan Fanshaw that her friend Tom Catchpole was a thief, and that her own daughter, along with Tom's son, had taken the sword and were probably at that very moment driving at full speed away from there.

Things out in the grounds had come on a long way during the morning. A number of stalls had been set up, the bare wooden frames gradually being covered with canvas and brightly coloured boards. Away over on one side a small funfair was under construction, the red and blue skeleton of a boat-swing ride already rising out of the chaos.

As the three girls went in search of Susan they noticed that the police tape had been taken off the chapel door.

'That's one small mystery solved,' Holly said softly. 'The police must have come and unsealed it this morning. That's why Tom went in there. It must have been the first chance he got.'

There was no sign of Tom, but they found Susan deep in animated conversation with three men in overalls with the word 'Bounce-Co' emblazoned on the back in big red letters.

'You tell us where you want it, lady, and we'll do the rest,' one of the men said.

'I'm not sure,' said Susan. She consulted a roughly drawn sketch map. 'How about over there?' she said, showing the map to the men.

'Fine,' said the man. 'As long as you don't mind us driving our lorry over your lawns.'

'I'm well past minding about things like that,' said Susan. The three men walked off and Susan caught sight of the girls.

She grinned tiredly at them. 'I'm frazzled!' she said. 'Every year I say: never again! But I always forget how mad it all gets. Have you come to help? That's very good of you. If you go and have a word with that chap over there, I'm sure he'll find something for you to do.' She pointed to a man with a clipboard surrounded by a crowd of people all talking at once.

'I'm afraid we've got some bad news,' Belinda said hesitantly.

Susan looked puzzled. 'I'm sorry? What do you

mean, dear? What sort of bad news?'

Belinda took a deep breath. This wasn't at all pleasant. 'It's about Lucy,' she said.

Susan frowned. 'I'm very busy, Belinda,' she said. 'I really think you're old enough to work through your problems with my daughter without coming to me.'

Holly felt a flush of embarrassment. Susan was bound to react badly to what they had to tell her, and even though they could prove Tom's role, there was still no real proof that Lucy was involved. She glanced over her shoulder, as if guided by some strange intuition. She let out a gasp of surprise.

'Susan's right,' Holly said suddenly, grabbing Belinda's arm and pulling her away. 'We shouldn't be bothering her with things like this now.'

'Hold on,' said Belinda, struggling in Holly's fierce grip. 'What are you doing?'

'Trust me!' said Holly. 'Tracy, come on, let's go and make ourselves useful.'

'Holly?' demanded Belinda. 'Will you tell me what this is all about?'

Holly towed Belinda out of earshot of Susan before pointing meaningfully towards the house.

Standing as large as life at the side of the house, talking to a small group of people and apparently perfectly calm and untroubled, was Lucy Fanshaw.

12 On the lookout

'What's she doing back here?' said Tracy as they stared in astonishment at Lucy Fanshaw. Holly and Belinda were thinking the same thing. Their carefully constructed theory had relied on the fact that Lucy and Colin had taken off with the stolen sword.

'If they've got the sword,' said Belinda, 'why is she still here?'

'This whole thing just gets more and more confusing,' said Holly. 'Maybe Colin's taken the sword away. Maybe she drove him somewhere with it this morning. Maybe he's going to sell it.'

'That's a lot of maybes,' said Belinda. 'And maybe we haven't got a clue what's going on here. What if Colin *is* going to sell the sword? What are they going to do with the money? Split it and carry on as if nothing has happened? We're talking about thousands and thousands of pounds.'

'Maybe they're planning to elope with it,' said Tracy.

'That would make sense, I suppose,' said Holly. 'If Colin is off right now, finding someone who is willing to buy the sword from them, then once he's got the money, he'll be back to pick Lucy up.'

'And that's when we'll nab them!' said Belinda. 'OK, here's the plan. On no account must we let Lucy out of our sight from now on. One of us must have her in plain view every minute of the day.'

'What about Tom Catchpole?' asked Tracy. 'Shouldn't we watch him, too? After all, he stole the sword in the first place.'

'Tracy's right, you know,' said Holly. 'If we've figured out that only Colin could get into that cross, then Tom's bound to have come to the same conclusion. And if he suspects Colin is involved, then it won't take him long to guess that Lucy is in on it as well. We need to watch both of them.'

'I can see that this is going to be quite an eventful day,' said Belinda.

'And with any luck we'll have the sword back for the Masquerade by the end of it,' said Holly.

'I seem to remember you saying something optimistic like that just before we almost got ourselves drowned last night,' said Belinda. 'In fact, if I remember correctly, the figure of ten million pounds was bet by someone round here whose name begins with an H and ends in Olly.'

'That's right,' said Tracy. 'You owe us ten million pounds, Holly.'

'I'll pay you the moment I get it,' said Holly. 'Just don't hold your breath!'

In the event Holly was proved wrong in her hopes, and Belinda's prediction about an eventful day was both wrong and right. The day was busy enough for the three girls. In fact they were kept so busy helping out with things that they found it quite difficult to keep a watch on Lucy.

But somehow they managed it, helped by the fact that Lucy spent most of the time wandering around chatting to people without ever actually making herself useful.

There was no sign of Tom Catchpole. Whatever his reaction to the shock of finding the Lady of Wrath missing, he certainly made himself scarce throughout that long, hot, exhausting day.

But by the middle of the evening, it seemed that everything that could be done had been done, except that over to the far right there was a steady hum of machinery as a large yellow and red bouncy castle slowly inflated against the darkening sky.

The last that the girls had seen of Lucy was

an hour or so ago when she had gone upstairs, presumably to her room.

They helped Susan prepare dinner, always keeping an ear open for any sound of Lucy coming back downstairs.

At about eight o'clock the men from Bounce-Co left and half an hour later the sound of a car in the drive announced the return of John Fanshaw.

'Any news of the Lady?' he asked Susan only moments after throwing his briefcase down and pouring himself a drink. Holly realised he was referring to the stolen sword.

'Nothing yet,' said Susan. 'But the police seem quite hopeful. The people at the museum are pretty angry, but I told them we did all we could. Tom is absolutely devastated by the whole thing. He blames himself.'

'It's not Tom's fault,' said John. The three girls looked at one another but said nothing.

'What do you think the thief will do with the sword?' asked Belinda.

'He's got two choices, really,' said John. 'If it was stolen by someone who knew what they were taking, then the chances are that it'll be sold to a private collector. Otherwise, the danger is that they'll just rip the jewels out of the hilt and throw the rest away.'

'And that would be a real tragedy,' said Susan.

'Well, there's nothing we can do about it,' said John. 'So let's not dwell on it.' He gave the three girls an unconvincing smile. 'I'm sure the police will find it. We might even have it back in time for the parade tomorrow night. I hope you're joining in. Have you picked out your costumes yet?'

'Sorry?' said Holly. 'What costumes?'

'It's my fault,' said Susan. 'I just took it for granted they'd want to join in. I completely forgot to ask them.' She looked at the three friends. 'Would you like to take part in the Masquerade? We've got plenty of spare costumes.'

'What do we have to do?' asked Belinda.

'All the young people gather at the top of the hill at nightfall with candles,' explained John. 'And then I come along, dressed up as Sir Brandon Wylde. I lead all the children down to the causeway. And then I have this little speech where I thank the lady of the river for giving me the sword, and finally all the children go along the causeway with their candles and pretend to be holding off the Parliamentarian Army.'

'Then everyone comes back up to the house for sausages and baked potatoes,' said Susan. 'And to watch the firework display and have some final rides at the funfair. It's great fun.' Her face fell.

'Or it would be if not for all this worry about the Lady.'

'We won't let it spoil our enjoyment,' said John. 'Well? Are you three up for it?'

'Just lead us to the costumes!' said Tracy.

'That can wait until the morning,' said Susan. 'I expect the three of you will be wanting your beds after all the hard work you've done today.'

'It was rather tiring,' admitted Holly. 'But we really enjoyed it.'

They went up to their bedrooms.

'OK,' said Holly. 'We've got to keep watch on Lucy all night. The same rota as last time. Belinda from now until two o'clock in the morning. Tracy from two 'til five, and me from then on.'

'Where do we watch from?' asked Belinda. 'And what exactly are we watching for her to *do*?'

'She's got to meet up with Colin at some stage,' said Holly. 'And my guess is that it'll be tonight. The moment she makes a move, whoever is on watch must alert the rest of us, and then we all go to Susan's bedroom and tell her the whole thing before Lucy has the chance to get away. That's the only way we're going to be able to convince Susan that we're not just making it all up because we don't like Lucy. She's got to be caught red-handed!'

* * *

It was to prove a long night for the three girls. They decided that their best course of action would be to hide in a small alcove up on the landing of the main staircase. A person could sit silently in there, out of sight, but able to see anyone who used the stairs.

Belinda managed to keep herself awake, although she was constantly nodding as the minutes crawled past. At two o'clock she plodded off to rouse Tracy.

'Anything?' whispered Tracy.

Belinda shook her head as she dragged herself sleepily off to bed. For the first half hour Tracy watched, poised and eager-eyed, but eventually the long silent hours of the night took their toll and by five o'clock, with the first pale light of dawn filtering through the windows, she woke Holly up with the news that nothing had happened so far.

And things stayed the same until about seven o'clock in the morning when Susan and John started moving about. As far as the three girls could tell, as they met wearily in Belinda's room, Lucy Fanshaw hadn't stirred a hair all night.

'I suppose she *is* still in her room?' asked Belinda. 'She couldn't have sneaked out through a window, could she?'

'I hadn't thought of that,' said Holly. 'I suppose we'd better check.'

They crept along to Lucy's closed bedroom door. Holly pressed her ear to the wood but there was no sound from within.

'What do we do?' whispered Belinda.

'Leave it to me,' said Tracy. Before either of her friends could say a word, she turned the handle and marched into the darkened bedroom.

'Hey, Belinda,' she shouted, 'time to get up! C'mon! Rise and shine! Oh! Lucy! I'm sorry. I thought this was Belinda's room. Wow, it's just so easy to get lost in this place, isn't it?' She backed out of the room and closed the door.

She grinned at her two friends. 'She's in there, all right,' she said. 'I think I woke her up.'

'She must think you're a total looney,' said Belinda. She looked at Holly. 'So what do we do now?'

'The only thing we *can* do,' Holly said determinedly. 'We keep watching her until she makes a move.'

They had a quick breakfast with John in the kitchen. Susan was already out organising the stallholders and fairground people who had arrived bright and early.

'When do we get to choose our costumes?' Tracy asked John.

'I'll show you where they're kept right now,' said John. 'Plenty of people spend the entire day dressed up, but it's up to you.' He looked distractedly at his watch. 'I wish I knew where Tom was. He should have been here by now to help finish setting up the firework display. And he's not at home either. I've tried ringing him several times.'

John took the three girls up to a room on the first floor. The walls were lined with cupboards filled with old clothes.

'They won't all be what you're looking for,' he told them. 'But you're bound to find something you like.'

He left them to it. Fortunately the windows of the room overlooked the front of the house and they could plainly see Lucy's sports car parked in the drive.

John was right about the clothing. It seemed to come from a lot of different periods in time. There were slinky, glittery dresses from the nineteen-twenties. There were huge, unwieldy Victorian crinolines, all smelling of mothballs and lavender.

'This looks more like it,' said Holly, pulling out a silvery-blue full-length dress with puffed sleeves and a high waistline. 'I'd look like someone from Camelot in this.'

'Hmm,' said Belinda, giving the dress the once over. 'Not really my type of thing, I don't think.' She dug around in the clothes and pulled out a costume with a green jacket and tights and a narrow, curved hat with a feather in it.

'Robin Hood!' she said. 'That'll do me. And green is my favourite colour, too!'

'But Robin Hood was a guy,' said Tracy.

'Says who? There's a girl at school called Robyn.'

'Yeah,' said Tracy. 'With a "y".'

'So they couldn't spell in those days.' said Belinda. 'Who cares? I'm going as Belinda Hood, and the next person who says anything about it gets an arrow up their nose!'

'This is nice,' said Tracy, drawing out a long, flowing green dress. It had full sleeves with extended, pointed cuffs that came down almost to the floor. The back of the dress spread out in heavy folds and the bodice was embroidered with brown and yellow leaves and flowers.

'Shall we put them on now?' said Holly. 'Or wait until this evening?'

'I don't know about you,' said Tracy, already half out of her jeans. 'But I'm changing right now.'

A few minutes later the three of them went down

to the main hall, Holly in her silvery-blue dress, Tracy in her green dress and Belinda defiant in her Robin Hood outfit.

Susan smiled at them as they stepped out of the back door. The four of them made their way across the garden to the busy festival area.

'You look wonderful,' she said. 'I'll go and put my own costume on soon. It's a pity Lucy can't get into the spirit of the thing. It was all I could do to get her to watch the raffle stall for me.' She nodded over to a nearby stall before being called away for something.

Lucy stood sullenly behind the stall, dressed in her ordinary black sweater and jeans.

'That's a bit of luck,' said Holly. 'It's not going to be difficult keeping an eye on her if she's stuck behind there most of the day.'

The fairground atmosphere was already beginning to grow. People were arriving in crowds, many of them in fancy dress, and music was playing over a loud-speaker system. Over to one side the turrets of the bouncy castle were wobbling as scores of small children leaped about on it, screaming and laughing at the tops of their voices.

The three girls were quickly found jobs to do. Belinda gave her friends a horrified look as she was led over to the bouncy castle to supervise the small children. Tracy helped out on a coconut shy and Holly got herself a job on a tombola stall within easy sight of Lucy.

Belinda managed to escape the leaping, bouncing, jumping and screaming children for a while in the middle of the day and the three of them met up at Holly's stall. Holly had nothing to report. Lucy had found herself a deckchair and was sitting sprawled out behind the stall, apparently engaged in nothing more suspicious than sunbathing.

One thing Holly was aware of, however, was the fact that John Fanshaw was still looking out for Tom Catchpole. The three friends knew perfectly well what had triggered his disappearance; they just wished they knew what he was doing.

Belinda and Tracy went back to their work for the long, hot, noisy afternoon. A lot of people were in fancy dress now, everything from Viking costumes to Beefeater uniforms and Roman togas. Holly noticed that most of the children and teenagers were dressed in Tudor-style clothes, presumably ready for their part in the Masquerade later that evening.

Belinda was exhausted. An entire day of rubbing bruised knees and looking after shoes and stopping tussles on the bouncy castle turning into major battles had worn her out. She found someone willing to take over from her and staggered off to get herself something to eat.

She stood in the queue of people waiting for a hot-dog. She had only been there a few seconds when something caught her eye. Someone was walking rapidly along behind the row of stalls. Someone with a grim and determined look on his face. Someone the three girls had been looking out for all day. Tom Catchpole!

Belinda left the queue and followed at a discreet distance. She could see that Tom was pursuing someone: a young blond-haired man who had just walked behind a tent, as though not wanting to be seen.

Belinda reached the tent. Both men had disappeared round the back, out of sight of the crowds. She leaned forwards and peered round the corner of canvas.

Tom Catchpole had caught the younger man and was holding him by the elbows. Even as Belinda ducked back out of sight, she heard Tom speak.

'OK, Colin,' he said, 'this has gone on long enough, boy. What have you and that girl done with the sword?'

Belinda drew a sharp breath. It looked as if things were finally coming to a head.

13 Deceit

'Well done!' said Holly as a small girl drew out one of the prize tickets from the tombola machine. She lifted the girl in her arms to show her the prizes from which she could choose.

'Wabbit!' said the girl, pointing a pudgy finger at a huge blue and white rabbit perched high on the stall.

'Wabbit is is,' said Holly. She put the child down and took the enormous rabbit down, smiling as mother and child wandered off, the little girl clutching the toy that was nearly as big as she was herself.

Holly glanced over at the stall where Lucy was supposedly helping out. All day Holly had been keeping watch, but the only time Lucy had even moved was to go and get herself something to eat in the early part of the afternoon. The rest of the time she had been either lounging in the deckchair with her eyes closed or reluctantly handing out raffle tickets to visitors.

It was beginning to get on Holly's nerves. Where was Colin? When were they going to make a move? The Mystery Club had finally hammered out a theory about the missing sword that seemed to fit all the facts *and* make sense. So why was nothing happening?

Holly dreamed up possibilities in her imagination. Perhaps Tom Catchpole had caught Colin before he could get rid of the sword. Perhaps Colin and Tom were working together and they'd both done a disappearing act with the sword, leaving Lucy high and dry. No, that didn't make any sense.

The only reason why Lucy should still be here, Holly decided, was because she and Colin were waiting for cover of night to slip away.

Holly thought about the P.J. Benson mystery books that she loved. How were things resolved in the Juliana Moon mysteries, for instance? There was one story, *The Reluctant Guest*, in which the young girl detective managed to panic the villains by confronting them with what she knew (but couldn't prove) and forcing them to act more quickly than they had intended.

Holly wondered if she could do something similar with Lucy. It might help to speed things up a little. If Lucy was in a panic she might make some mistake that would give the Mystery Club all the information it needed to prove her link to the theft of the Lady of Wrath.

Holly left the tombola stall for a few moments, determined to confront Lucy. The young woman was lying in the deckchair behind her stall, eyes closed and hands folded on her stomach.

Holly crouched by her side. 'Lucy?'

The bright blue eyes opened a slit. 'What?'

Holly noticed something that intrigued her. Lucy's hands were spattered with small stains of some black substance, and there was more blackness under her fingernails. Not dirt or grime, but something more like black paint.

'We know what's been going on,' Holly said softly. 'We know all about the sword and everything. I think you should give it back. Do that, and I promise we won't say a word to anyone. You can tell your parents that you found it. We won't tell on you.'

'I don't have the faintest idea what you're talking about,' said Lucy, closing her eyes. 'Why don't you go and play on the cliffs with your little friends? Right near the edge, preferably!'

'Tom knows you swapped the swords,' said Holly. 'Do you think he's going to let you get away with that?'

The colour drained from Lucy's face but she said nothing. Holly leaned a little closer to her ear. 'If I were you, I'd be getting very worried,' she whispered. 'What are you going to do if Tom has already found Colin?'

Lucy's eyes opened, staring straight into Holly's, and from the confusion and doubt in Lucy's gaze, Holly could tell that her words had had a huge effect on the young woman.

Holly stood up and walked back to her own stall. Lucy was staring at her as if she couldn't decide whether to fly at her or make a run for it.

An amplified voice came over the loudspeaker system.

'Will everyone involved in the Children's Masquerade please start making their way to the front of the house.'

The long day of festivities was almost at an end. The sun was an orange ball low on the horizon and lengthening shadows were stretching over the grounds of Wylde House. But there was still a lot going on. The small fairground was a maelstrom of noise and activity, and plenty of people were still wandering among the stalls or sitting in groups on the grass eating hot-dogs and ice-creams.

Black paint.

Holly was certain that there was some significance in the fact that Lucy had black paint on her fingers. She searched her memory, trying to recall where she had heard paint mentioned recently. And then it came to her, all in a rush.

It had been in the armoury, the first time that Holly had heard Lucy and Colin speaking. Someone had mentioned something about paint, about having the paint ready. But for what? It had to be something to do with the theft of the sword.

Holly let out an involuntary gasp as the truth suddenly flicked into clear focus in her head.

'Got it!' she said to herself. 'Of *course*!' And if she was right, then the answer to the whole mystery was still to be found in Wylde House.

No wonder no one had been seen fleeing with the sword. The sword was still there! And if Holly's suspicions were correct, she knew exactly where it was.

Belinda kept out of sight as Colin struggled to get free of his father's grasp.

'I haven't done anything,' said Colin. 'I haven't got the sword.'

'No, but you know where it is, don't you?' said Tom. 'I should have guessed there was something fishy going on when you phoned me. When have you ever bothered phoning for a chat, eh? I should have known you weren't in Manchester.'

'OK, OK,' gasped Colin. 'Look, it was all Lucy's idea. I just went along with her.' The tone of his voice changed. 'But we don't need her, Dad. We can have the sword between us. We can forget all about her.'

'Keep talking,' said Tom, his fingers still clutching his son's collar.

'She never intended to really steal the sword at all,' said Colin. 'That's what's so funny about the whole thing. She was angry with her father for forcing her to go to university when she wanted to stay here with me. So she came up with this plan where it would look like the sword had been stolen. Her idea was that she'd pretend to *find* the sword. Do you get it? Then her father would realise she wasn't just a dumb kid who could be ordered about. If her father could be conned into believing that she was bright enough to find the stolen sword, then he'd let her make her own mind up about university.'

'So how was this plan supposed to work?' asked Tom.

'Lucy found a secret passage between the armoury and the chapel,' said Colin. 'She discovered it years ago, when she was a kid, but she never told anyone. It was her secret place, where she'd go when she wanted to be on her own. So she could get into the chapel without setting off your alarm. But then when she told me her idea about hiding the sword, I looked through your files and found out the code so she could let me into the chapel without the alarm going off. It was safer for her to let me into the house that way, through the passage.' Colin took a deep breath. Belinda was flattened against the canvas side of the tent, hardly breathing as she took in every word the young man spoke.

'We were going to take the sword a couple of nights before the Masquerade,' Colin continued. 'The plan was that we'd hide it, and then she'd bring it out at the last moment, just before the kids march down to the river. She was going to hand it to her dad in front of all of them. But as soon as it went missing I knew you must be involved.'

'How did you know that?' growled Tom.

'I saw you making that cross, don't forget,' said Colin. 'I knew it was hollow, and I knew how the back opened. It didn't take long to figure out what you'd done.'

'So you took it,' said Tom. 'And now that stupid girl is going to give it back to John Fanshaw.' He shook Colin angrily. 'I need that sword,' Colin. I know someone who'll pay a lot of money for it – money I need if I'm not going to go bankrupt.'

'Bankrupt?' said Colin. 'I didn't know you had money problems.'

'You do now,' said Tom. 'You're going to get that sword for me from wherever you and that girl have hidden it.'

'Yes, OK,' said Colin. 'I'll take you there right now. Dad, trust me, I don't even like Lucy Fanshaw. I always meant to get the sword for myself and sell it.' Colin's voice became wheedling. 'But now we can have the money between us. You can solve your money problems and I can use my half of the money to get myself an air ticket to America. I've always wanted to live in America. Dad? What do you say, is it a deal?'

'Where's the sword?' asked Tom.

'Not far,' said Colin. 'Let go of me, and I'll show you.'

Belinda wasn't certain of exactly what happened next. There was a scuffle and an angry shout from Tom and the next thing Belinda saw was the young man running at full tilt out from behind the tent. Tom came charging after him, but he miscalculated the jump over the guy-rope that stretched out from the corner of the tent. Tom tripped and staggered, crashing into

Belinda and sending both of them tumbling to the ground.

The last thing Belinda saw as she fell was Colin's back merging into the crowd.

Tom quickly dragged himself to his feet. He gave Belinda a devastating glare and for a moment she thought he was going to hit her. But then he stared into the crowd for a moment, his teeth gritted in an angry snarl, before turning and running along behind the nearby hot-dog stall.

Belinda pulled herself together. She had aching ribs from the collision with Tom, and her shoulder hurt from the fall, but she had no time to worry about things like that. She had to get to Holly and Tracy as quickly as possible.

She dodged through the crowds, heading for the coconut shy where Tracy was helping out. She didn't waste a moment in explanations. Explanations could wait until the three of them were together. She simply grabbed hold of Tracy's wrist and yanked her out from behind the shy like pulling a cork out of a bottle.

'What the heck is happening?' Tracy gasped as Belinda hauled her through the throng of people. 'Is Holly in trouble?'

'No,' panted Belinda. 'But I've seen Tom. And Colin. And I know what's been going on.'

'Wait!' insisted Tracy, 'I can't run in this dress!' The long folds of the dress were wrapping themselves round her legs, threatening to trip her over. She grabbed swathes of material in either hand and followed after Belinda, holding the train of the dress up out of the way of her feet.

'Holly!' gasped Belinda as she reached the tombola stall. 'Tom Catchpole! Colin! The sword!' And then Belinda stared past Holly. 'Where's Lucy?' she yelled.

Holly spun round. The deckchair over at Lucy's stall was empty. There was no sign of the young woman.

'She's only just gone,' said Holly. 'I spoke to her a few seconds ago.'

Tracy came running up. 'What's happening?' she asked.

Belinda gabbled out a rapid version of what she had overheard behind the tent. 'I lost sight of Colin in among all the people,' she said. 'And Tom ran off round the backs of the stalls. He was heading this way. I thought he'd be looking for Lucy.'

'Lucy's gone!' said Tracy. 'Do you think he got her?'

'Not without someone seeing,' said Holly. 'Quick, you two, I think I know where she might have gone. And I think I know where the Lady of Wrath is!'

Holly didn't leave any time for a discussion as she ran across the gardens towards the house with Belinda and Tracy close behind.

Evening shadows were beginning to merge as the bright orange rim of the sun slid out of sight. The sky darkened over the cliffs. Holly led her two friends in through the back door of the house. It was cooler in here, and much quieter.

'Where are we going?' asked Tracy.

'To the armoury,' said Holly. 'The Lady of Wrath is in there.'

'How did you find out?' panted Belinda.

'From Lucy,' said Holly as she ran out of the kitchen and turned into the corridor that would take them into the north wing.

'She *told* you?' said Tracy. 'Just like that?'

'*She* didn't,' said Holly. 'Her hands did.'

'Holly Adams!' exclaimed Belinda. 'Will you please start making sense!'

'In a minute,' said Holly. 'Let's get there first.'

Holly came to a halt in the corridor a few metres before they came to the open armoury door. She motioned to the other two to keep quiet as she crept nearer to the room.

Tracy and Belinda gazed at each other in baffled silence as Holly slid her head round the edge of the door.

'It's OK,' said Holly. 'I thought she might already be here, but she isn't.' She walked into the long room, already shadowy in the twilight.

'Shall I switch the light on?' said Belinda.

'No, not yet,' said Holly. 'Belinda? Keep by the door. Let us know if anyone comes. Tracy, will you help me with a couple of these chests?'

Belinda kept watch by the door as Tracy and Holly lifted one of the smaller chests and, under Holly's instructions, carried it over to the fireplace.

'What are we doing?' asked Tracy.

'You'll see,' said Holly, going over to the other small chest. 'Come on, this should do it,' she said.

Tracy shook her head as she bent to grasp the side handle of the chest. 'I hope you know what you're doing,' she said.

They put the chest on top of the first one.

Holly climbed up on to the chests, balancing herself against the high mantelpiece.

Tracy watched from below as Holly stared up at the fan shaped set of black metal swords that were displayed on the chimney breast.

'Got it!' said Holly. 'I knew it!' She took hold of the hilt of one of the swords and carefully lifted it out of its brackets. It was surprisingly heavy and unwieldy and she nearly lost balance as the weight of the sword pulled her arms down.

'Can you give me a hand?' she called down to Tracy.

Between them, the two girls got the sword down safely and Holly jumped to the floor.

'This is the Lady of Wrath,' she said. 'Lucy and Colin painted it black to disguise it.'

Belinda came over to them and crouched to stare at the sword as it lay on the floor.

'Crumbs!' breathed Belinda. 'You're right! It's really obvious from close up.' The jewelled hilt was coated with a thick layer of black paint, as was the length of the once-silver blade. From a distance the paint made the sword seem no different from the others that were fixed to the wall.

'How the heck did you figure it out?' said Tracy.

'Lucy mentioned something about paint to Colin the first time I heard them speak to each other,' said Holly. 'I almost forgot about it until I noticed this afternoon that Lucy's hands had black paint on them.' She looked at Tracy. 'Remember that you were wondering in the chapel why anyone would substitute a different sword for the Lady of Wrath? That was the final clue. If they were going to hide the Lady in amongst the other swords on the wall, then they had to find somewhere else to put the one that was up here originally.' Holly's eyes gleamed as she spoke. 'Where better to hide it than back in the cross? Lucy and Colin must have done all this the night we were sent off to the watch tower.'

'But Colin told his father that Lucy never intended to really steal the sword,' said Belinda. 'Her plan was to give it back to him this evening, and pretend that she'd worked out where it had been hidden. That's what Colin said, anyway.'

'Lucy said you three were a pain in the neck. I can see what she meant now!' The voice came suddenly out of the shadows. As the three girls stared in shock towards the end of the room, Colin Catchpole stepped into the armoury and closed the door behind him.

The girls stood up. Colin was wearing thick gloves and was carrying something in his hand, although they couldn't make out what it was.

'Where's Lucy?' asked Holly.

'I don't know, and I don't care,' said Colin. 'I've come for the sword.' He grinned coldly. 'Thanks for taking it down for me.'

'You're not going to give the sword back, are you?' said Belinda. 'You never intended to go along with Lucy's plan. You just used her.'

'Lucy's an idiot,' said Colin. 'A nice enough idiot, but an idiot all the same. That sword is going to take me a long way from here. A long way from Lucy, and from my father.'

'Do you really think we're going to stand here and let you walk out with it?' said Tracy.

'That's exactly what I think you're going to do,' said Colin. He pulled something out of his pocket. It was the long tube of a firework. A Roman candle. He grasped it by one end in his gloved hand and pointed it towards the girls. 'Do you know what would happen if I lit this while I had it aimed at you?' he said. 'Have you ever seen the sort of damage a firework can do if it gets you in the face?'

'You wouldn't dare,' said Tracy.

'No?' Colin lifted his other hand and now they saw what he was holding. It was a cigarette lighter. He flicked his thumb and a pale yellow flame flickered.

'Now,' he said as he drew the dancing flame closer to the touchpaper at the end of the firework. 'Back away from the sword or I'll set this off. I'm not playing games. If you don't get away from that sword you're going to regret it.'

Holly swallowed her fear. From the look in his

eyes, Colin seemed quite capable of setting that firework off in their faces.

'I think we'd better do as he says,' said Holly.

The three girls backed slowly away from the sword as Colin advanced on them. They didn't seem to have any other choice.

14 Fire and water

Colin crouched by the sword, his eyes on the three girls. He was still holding the lighter flame close to the end of the firework. Holly licked her dry lips. In the next few seconds Colin would have to put down either the firework or the cigarette lighter in order to be able to pick up the sword. She was trying to decide whether there would be time for the three of them to rush him in those few moments when the direct threat of having the firework set off in their faces was lifted.

There was a sound from the end of the room. Colin glanced over his shoulder as Lucy opened the armoury door and came into the twilit room. Her eyes widened in surprise as she saw Colin crouched on the floor, holding the three girls at bay.

'Colin?' she gasped. 'What's going on?'

'It's OK,' said Colin. 'Come here. Quick!'

Lucy ran across to him.

'Pick the sword up,' said Colin.

'What are we going to do?' Lucy's voice was desperate. She stared at the three girls. 'I hate you,' she spat. 'You've ruined everything!'

'He was never going to let you give the sword back!' said Belinda. 'He was going to take it and dump you.'

'Just shut up,' said Lucy. 'You don't know anything!' She looked down at the young man. 'The procession has just started,' she said. 'I can still get the sword back to my father in time. If these three say anything I'll just tell him they're lying. My father will believe me, I'm sure he will.' She looked imploringly at Colin. 'It's still going to work, I'm sure it is.' Her voice was getting more and more shrill. 'I could even tell him they stole it!'

'Just pick the sword up, Lucy,' said Colin. 'Pick it up and go to the door.'

Lucy hefted the long sword in both hands.

'You idiot!' yelled Tracy. 'He's not doing this so you two can be together. He's going to sell you out, Lucy!'

'I don't believe you,' said Lucy.

Colin backed towards the door, still holding the firework and the lighter close together as he and Lucy moved away from Holly and the others.

'Is there a key to this door?' Colin asked Lucy. 'Is there some way of locking them in here?'

Lucy shook her head.

'OK,' said Colin. 'Listen to me, Lucy, and do exactly what I say. Where is your car?'

'It's parked at the front,' said Lucy. 'But why? We don't need—'

'Just shut up and listen!' snapped Colin. 'Take the sword. Go to your car and start it up. I'll follow you.'

Lucy seemed taken aback at the violence in Colin's voice. For a moment she hesitated, her eyes flickering from him to the three girls.

'We don't need the car, Colin,' she said confusedly. 'Not if we're going to give the sword back to my father.'

'Do what I tell you,' said Colin. 'Trust me. I'll explain everything as soon as I've dealt with these three. Now go!'

Lucy gave Colin a final, anxious glance, then slid through the half-open door.

'When are you going to tell her the truth?' asked Tracy.

Colin grinned savagely. 'I think she'll figure it out when I drive out of here,' he said. He looked coldly at them. 'I think you need teaching a lesson about keeping your noses out of other people's business.'

'You couldn't teach a fish to swim!' said Belinda.

'Just because you can scare Lucy, don't think you can frighten us.'

'Yeah,' said Tracy. 'We've been threatened by experts, knuckle-head. You're about as scary as a snowflake!'

'Is that so?' said Colin. Almost before they realised what was happening, Colin had touched the lighter flame to the end of the firework. There was a hiss and a fizzle of white sparks. Colin threw the Roman candle at them and ducked out through the door.

'Watch out!' yelled Holly. The spluttering firework spun through the air, shedding white arrowheads of fire.

The girls scattered as the Roman candle hit the floor. If the lit end was to brush against Holly or Tracy's floor-length dresses, their clothing could go up in flames. It skidded towards Belinda and she let out a yell, kicking it away. It whirled around as it slid over the boards, the spitting growing into a fierce hiss as a plume of white fire erupted from the end.

The firework came to rest against the wall, spewing thick red smoke and a flare of scarlet flame.

'The curtains!' shouted Holly. They could see why she had yelled. The blazing flame was close to the trailing edge of a curtain. Another few seconds and there would be the very real danger of the material catching light.

'Keep back!' said Belinda. She ran forwards, circling round to the back of the firework and giving it a shove with her foot. She managed to angle the flame away from the wall. The flame roared as she nudged the Roman candle back into the middle of the room. The thick red smoke billowed up around her as she stamped down hard across the firework. The brightly coloured flame spluttered and died.

They stared at each other in relief as the dense acrid smoke rose around them.

'Colin!' yelled Holly. 'Quick!'

They ran helter-skelter out of the armoury and down the corridors to the front of the house. The front door was wide open as Holly came racing out.

Madrigal music was playing over the loudspeaker system away over to her right and she could see a winding line of children making their way down the hillside towards the bridge. The line was spangled with tiny tongues of white light where each of the children carried a candle in a bottle.

But it was to the left that her attention was drawn. There was Lucy's sports car, and standing at the open driver's door was Colin. Even as Holly and the others ran towards the car, Colin heaved backwards, pulling Lucy out of the car and sending her sprawling in the gravel.

'Colin! *No*!' Lucy screamed as the young man forced his way into the driver's seat and slammed the door.

The motor revved and the car leaped forwards, going over the edge of the flat gravel driveway and angling downwards as the wheels came on to the grass.

Holly couldn't see the sword, but she realised it must be in the car. And she could guess what Colin intended. The line of the Children's Masquerade was on the road, about two thirds of the way towards the bridge. He was going to drive across the grassy slope of the hill in the hope of reaching the bridge before them and escaping along the causeway.

Lucy leaped to her feet and chased after the car, screaming at Colin to stop. But it wasn't Lucy's screams that brought the sports car to a sudden halt, it was another vehicle which came careering out from the side of the house away from the road.

It was an open-backed Land-Rover, spraying gravel from its wheels as it churned across the drive and bounced over on to the slope. Holly saw Tom

Catchpole's face, contorted with rage as he wrestled the wheel around. The Land-Rover skidded to a halt full in the path of the sports car.

The sports car almost crashed into the side of the Land-Rover before Colin was able to slam on the brakes and come to a slewing halt.

Tom was out of the Land-Rover in a split second, his feet sliding on the grass as he ran to the driver's door of the sports car and wrenched it open.

As Holly and the others watched in amazement, Tom struggled briefly with Colin before pulling back from the car with the long sword clutched in both hands.

'Stop them!' screamed Lucy. 'Please! Someone do something!'

'Call the police!' shouted Belinda as she ran past Lucy. Holly was directly ahead of her, running in Tracy's wake towards the two vehicles.

But none of them was quick enough to stop Tom as he threw the sword into the front of the Land-Rover and jumped in after it. Tracy went skidding down the slope to the front of the Land-Rover, trying to catch hold of the door handle. But she was a moment too late. Even as her hands snatched at thin air, Tom stamped down on the accelerator and the Land-Rover sprang forwards down the hill.

But Tracy wasn't going to give in that easily.

She made a lunge for the side of the Land-Rover, gripping the edge of the back with both hands. She was swept off her feet, but clung on grimly, managing to hook a foot up over the side.

The Land-Rover bounced and battered her as she swung herself up into the relative safety of its open back. She tumbled among planks and poles, still clinging on to the side as the vehicle went plunging down the hillside.

Holly stared in horror as she saw her friend carried helplessly away in the speeding Land-Rover. There was nothing she could do to help, the Land-Rover was already a long way down the hill and gathering speed all the time.

But she could make sure Colin didn't get away. He was halfway out of the sports car, staring down at the Land-Rover as if things had happened too quickly for him to take in.

'Belinda! Get him!' shouted Holly.

The two girls ran for the sports car. Colin pulled himself back in, but wasn't quite quick enough. Belinda jammed her foot in the door and the two girls jerked it open, half-dragging Colin out of the seat as he tried to stop them.

Colin sprawled in the grass. Belinda trod on him as she leaned into the car to grab the keys. But the car made a sudden lurch forwards.

Holly saw Belinda's peril immediately. The handbrake couldn't have been put on and Belinda's weight on the car had started it rolling down the hill. Holly let out a shriek of warning and sprang forwards. Her fingers closed on the back of Belinda's tunic and she pulled her friend clear.

Holly, Belinda and Colin lay dazedly in the grass as the sports car gathered speed down the hill towards the distant dark line of the river.

Tracy had just enough left of her scattered wits to wonder how on earth she had got herself into this situation. Tom was driving the bucking Land-Rover faster and faster down the hill and it was all his unwanted passenger could do to keep herself from being flung out of the back along with all the pieces of wood that were spilling in their wake.

She managed to keep hold of the metal edge of the back. If she lost her grip she'd be tossed out like a rag-doll. She lifted her head above the edge. The evening was darkening and she saw that the head of the candlelit line of the Children's Masquerade was almost at the bridge.

Tom slammed his fist down on the horn again and again, sending out raucous blasts of noise above the clarion of the music brodcast from the top of the hill. Tracy saw the children looking round. She saw panic on their faces as the Land-Rover sped towards them. She saw the line waver and break up as the children scattered in terror. And she saw one tall figure in shining armour standing at the near end of the narrow bridge, looking for all the world in the dark of the late evening like a white knight in a fairy story.

It's John Fanshaw, Tracy thought. *He's dressed up like Sir Brandon Wylde!*

The horn of the Land-Rover blared continuously now as the costumed children fled from the road. But John Fanshaw didn't move. He stood foursquare in the centre of the road and spread his arms out.

For a terrible moment Tracy was sure Tom would simply run him over, but at the last possible moment the Land-Rover went skidding to one side, missing John by a hair's-breadth.

The whole world went crazy for a moment as Tracy was flung about in the back. Then the Land-Rover nose-dived and came to a stunning halt that sent her crashing into the back of the cab in a tangle of arms and legs.

A cascade of water came pouring down over Tracy. The Land-Rover was at a mad angle, as though standing on its nose. Spluttering and totally disorientated, Tracy stumbled to her feet. The Land-Rover had slid down the bank of the River Wrath and was half-submerged in the dark water.

The driver's door sprang open and Tom Catchpole almost fell out, knee-deep in the water. He was holding the Lady of Wrath, trying to pull it out of the cab without losing his footing.

Tracy took two lungfuls of air and screamed at the top of her voice. Tom jumped almost clear of the river in shock. His fingers lost grip of the sword hilt and the Lady of Wrath slid down between his feet into the swirling water.

Tom's eyes fixed on Tracy with murderous intent. He snarled and started climbing up the side of the Land-Rover towards her.

'Don't touch me!' Tracy yelled as she tried to scramble away from him. She managed to get to the far side of the Land-Rover. She balanced precariously for a moment on the narrow edge, hoping that she had the strength in her legs to leap clear of the water.

Just as she jumped, Tom's fingers caught the trailing end of her long dress. She felt a powerful wrench pull her to one side as her foot slipped and she fell.

She had only a split second to fill her lungs with air before she hit the water and sank down and down into the chilling depths of the fast-running River Wrath.

15 The Lady returns

From her vantage point at the top of the hill, Holly saw the whole thing. Her heart leaped into her throat as she saw the Land-Rover heading straight for the line of children. She saw them running in all directions and saw the tiny figure of John Fanshaw blocking the bridge.

Belinda picked herself up, her fingers digging into Holly's arm as they watched the Land-Rover swerve and career towards the river. They could just see Tracy's blonde head bobbing in the back.

'Hold on, Tracy!' hissed Belinda. And then the Land Rover slid nose-first down the steep riverbank and a spray of white water came gushing up.

'Come on!' shouted Holly. 'We've got to help her!'

They ran down the hillside, occasionally slipping and almost falling as they sped to help Tracy.

The sports car was rumbling down the hill to their left. Going faster and faster until it reached the river. It arched out into the air before crashing into the water. The front of the car must have got lodged in thick mud, because it didn't topple over, but just stood there with its back high out of the water.

Holly and Belinda saw Tracy fall from the Land-Rover and heard the splash of her hitting the water.

John Fanshaw was running along the riverbank, shouting something that they couldn't understand.

Tom Catchpole climbed to the back of the Land-Rover and jumped down into the grass.

'Get him!' screamed Belinda. 'He stole the sword!'

Tom had fallen awkwardly and as he tried to stand, his leg seemed to give way beneath him.

John Fanshaw came down on Tom like a ton of bricks, flattening him into the grass and pulling an arm up behind him to prevent Tom from getting away.

'You maniac!' John shouted in a fury. 'You could have killed someone!'

'Don't let him go!' gasped Holly. 'He stole the Lady of Wrath.'

'Tracy!' yelled Belinda. 'Where's Tracy?'

She scrambled down alongside the precariously balanced Land-Rover and searched the river for their missing friend. The water flowed smooth and dark. There was no sign of Tracy.

'Look upstream,' called John. 'The tide's coming in. She might have been swept along with it.'

Holly joined Belinda at the grassy edge. There was a long fall of brown mud between them and the low, swirling waters of the river.

'Tracy!' shouted Holly as she searched desperately for some sight of the girl.

'She's a brilliant swimmer,' said Belinda. 'She'll be all right.'

'In that dress?' gasped Holly. 'And in all this mud? I can't see her! I can't see her anywhere!'

'Look!' Belinda almost screamed. She pointed down to the river directly in front of them.

Something was stirring in the water. And then a blonde head broke the surface and Tracy's face appeared. She spat out a long spume of river water as her shoulders came clear of the tide.

'I'm OK!' she coughed. 'I've got it!'

They saw her struggle with something and a second later the long, black blade of the Lady of Wrath clove up through the waters, clutched securely in Tracy's two hands.

Using the sword as a prop, Tracy struggled to the river's edge. Holly and Belinda reached down for her and a few hectic moments later the three of them were hugging one another on the bank.

'Good heavens!' gasped John Fanshaw, staring at Tracy. 'The prophecy came true!'

'Huh?' said Tracy, pulling saturated hair out of her eyes.

'Of course!' said Holly. 'The prophecy about the Lady of Wrath. The river-woman said that if the sword was ever taken by force from Sir Brandon's hand, she'd come back to retrieve it.'

'Yeah? Right, so?' said Tracy.

'Don't you remember what the legend said she looked like?' said Belinda. 'Golden hair and a long green dress. Tracy! It's *you*!'

A broad grin spread itself over Tracy's face. 'Wow!' she said. 'I'm a legend!' And at that moment, as if in confirmation of her words, there was a huge blossom of light high in the sky and a reverberating cymbal-crash of thunder as the firework display began.

The police were there within minutes. Lucy had obeyed Belinda's yell way back at the top of the hill, and she had run to the house and called them on the telephone.

Holly gave the police a quick explanation of what had happened while John, Tracy and Belinda helped round up the frightened children and herded them back up to the house.

Tom and Colin were arrested on the spot. Lucy came walking slowly down the hill, her head hanging.

'I think you'd better come with us, miss,' said one of the police officers.

'I never meant to steal it, Daddy,' said Lucy, looking imploringly into her father's eyes. 'I just wanted you to think I was grown up enough to make up my own mind about university.' She stared briefly at Colin through the police car window. 'I've been so stupid!' she said. 'Daddy? Forgive me, please?'

Her father gazed sadly at her then took her in his arms. He looked at the police officer.

'I'll bring Lucy in to the station in the morning,' he said. 'You'll get a full statement out of her then.'

Holly and Belinda marched the soaking wet Tracy up to the house and all three of them changed back into their ordinary clothes before going out into the gardens to watch the firework display with the rest of the crowds. The shock of the arrests had been lessened by the fact that the Lady of Wrath had been found. The Children's Masquerade, despite the disruption, ended relatively cheerfully when a long set-piece firework display spelt out the words GOODNIGHT, EVERYONE in blazing white letters.

Holly and her friends sat with Lucy, John and Susan. Lucy was very quiet and subdued, silently holding her parents' hands. The discovery that Colin was simply using her to get the sword had stunned her.

But as the evening came to an end and the crowds began to disperse, Lucy stood up and walked over to Holly and her friends.

'I want to apologise for everything,' she said. 'I've been terrible to you ever since you came here. I feel such a fool!' She looked over her shoulder at her parents. 'I've made one sensible decision tonight at least,' she said. 'I'm going to take up the place I was offered at university.'

'How long have you known about the secret passage?' asked Belinda.

'For years,' said Lucy. 'I found it when I was a child. It was my secret place. The only person I ever told about it was Colin. I thought I could trust him!' She sighed. 'That just shows how good a judge of people I am!'

'And what about the room?' asked Tracy.

Lucy looked puzzled. 'What room?'

'I told you they didn't know anything about it,' said Belinda. 'You could see that place hadn't been explored for ages.' She looked at Lucy. 'There's a doorway in the passage,' she said. 'It leads up to the priest's hole. We've been up there.'

'What's this?' asked John. 'A secret room as well as a secret passage?'

'That's right,' said Holly. 'But I'm afraid there's no treasure. It's just a bare little room.'

John looked round at Susan. 'I don't care if it is a bare room,' he said. 'I want to see it.' He looked at the three friends. 'Can you take me there?'

'What?' said Holly. 'You mean now?'

'I certainly do,' said John. 'Right now!'

Holly led the group up to the priest's hole. John had given her a powerful torch to show the way. The six of them, Holly, Tracy and Belinda, and Susan, John and Lucy, just about fitted into the tiny slope-roofed room.

'I must have stepped over that bar hundreds of times,' said Lucy. 'I never dreamed it was anything to do with another doorway.'

'We're just sorry the room's not stuffed with treasure,' said Belinda. 'I suppose Oliver Cromwell's army must have taken it all away after all.' She shuffled across the floor and sat on the edge of the long wooden box-construction that lay against the wall. 'We've already had one legend come true tonight,' she said. 'I suppose it's a bit much to expect Lady Eleanor's treasure to simply – oh, crumbs!' As she put her full weight on the old timbers, there was a dry cracking sound and she found herself back on the floor in a flurry of splinters.

'Belinda!' shrieked Tracy.

'I'm sorry,' said Belinda. 'I didn't mean to – what? What? What's everyone staring . . . at . . . ohhh!' Belinda looked down. Amongst the splinters and shards of wood something gold was gleaming. Everyone gazed at it as Holly swept the torch downwards.

Gold coins spilled out of the box, glinting in the torchlight.

'The treasure!' yelled Tracy. 'Oh, my Lord! Belinda's found the treasure!'

No one got much sleep that night. It took the six of them over an hour to carry all the treasures down out of the secret room and out into the armoury.

The old bedstead had been crammed with beautiful, priceless things. Silver plates and cups. Knives and forks and candlesticks, all of solid silver, black with age but worth a fortune. And then they had found a box filled with jewels and brooches and necklaces, as well as several bags of gold coins like the one that had split when Belinda had sat on it.

But what seemed to excite John the most was a small box full of old letters. Letters from King Charles the First to Sir Brandon.

'These will probably be worth more than all the rest put together,' he said, gazing at the crinkly brown parchment. 'Letters like this are selling for vast amounts in London auctions!' he gazed, wide-eyed at the others. 'I think we're going to be very, very well off.'

'Hey,' said Tracy. 'Does this mean you'll be able to afford to do the work so you can open Wylde House up for the public?'

Susan and John looked at each other.

'I think so,' said John. 'And I can't think of a more perfect use for Lady Eleanor's treasure.' He gazed around at the treasures that lay spread out on the armoury floor as if he was afraid his eyes were playing tricks on him. 'I can't quite believe it yet,' he said. 'It's like a miracle.'

'Oh, you'll get used to it,' Belinda said with a big grin. 'Things like this are always happening when the Mystery Club is around!'

THE MYSTERY CLUB SERIES
FIONA KELLY

58867 5	Secret Clues	☐
58868 3	Double Danger	☐
58869 1	Forbidden Island	☐
58870 5	Mischief at Midnight	☐
59283 4	Dangerous Tricks	☐
59284 2	Missing!	☐
60723 8	Hide and Seek	☐
60724 6	Buried Secrets	☐
60725 4	Deadly Games	☐
60726 2	Crossed Lines	☐
60727 0	Dark Horse	☐
60728 9	Deceptions	☐
63609 2	Fatal Fall	☐
63610 6	Crash Landing!	☐
63611 4	Poison!	☐
63612 2	Out of Control	☐

All Hodder Children's books are available at your local bookshop or newsagent, or can be ordered direct from the publisher. Just tick the titles you want and fill in the form below. Prices and availability subject to change without notice.

Hodder Children's Books, Cash Sales Department, Bookpoint, 39 Milton Park, Abingdon, OXON, OX14 4TD, UK. If you have a credit card you may order by telephone – 01235 831700.

Please enclose a cheque or postal made payable to Bookpoint Ltd to the value of the cover price and allow the following for postage and packing:
UK & BFPO – £1.00 for the first book 50p for the second book, and 30p for each additional book ordered up to a maximum charge of £3.00.
OVERSEAS & EIRE – £2.00 for the first book, £1.00 for the second book, and 50p for each additional book.

Name ....

Address ....

....

....
If you would prefer to pay by credit card, please complete:
Please debit my Visa/Access/Diner's Card/American Express (delete as applicable) card no:

Signature ....

Expiry Date ....